RAVE REVIEWS FOR *THE NIGHT CLASS* AND TOM PICCIRILLI!

WINNER OF THE BRAM STOKER AWARD!

"Piccirilli is, bar none, one of the best writers working in the field today."
—*Mindmares*

"Loaded with grim characters, an unusual plot, and a murky, almost surreal atmosphere, *The Night Class* is a must-read for fans of the macabre."
—*Masters of Terror*

"Tom Piccirilli's work is full of wit and inventiveness—sharp as a sword, tart as apple vinegar. I look forward to all his work."
—Joe R. Lansdale, author of *Mucho Mojo*

"A hyperventilating horror mystery. *The Night Class* draws on the venerable tradition of stories that plumb the unbridgeable gulf between school learning and life lessons."
—*Publishers Weekly*

"*The Night Class* has characters, plot, and story that all work beautifully—but the atmosphere works best of all. A first-rate book."
—Ed Gorman, author of *The Dark Fantastic*

MORE ACCLAIM FOR TOM PICCIRILLI!

"A gifted and imaginative author. Piccirilli's is a matter-of-fact world of magic and demons and ghosts, a world any Clive Barker fan would recognize."
—Bentley Little, *Hellnotes*

"Tom Piccirilli delivers the goods. I'm a big fan."
—Richard Laymon, author of *Night in the Lonesome October*

"If you don't know the brilliant Mr. Piccirilli, you should. He makes you believe in his magic, in much the same way H. P. Lovecraft made us believe in his Mythos, and he can scare the hell out of you."
–Brian McNaughton, author of *Throne of Bones*

"Piccirilli splices genres, combining elements of supernatural horror with hardboiled fiction to produce a narrative that sizzles. This is whiplash fiction that takes dangerous curves at 150 m.p.h."
—*Deathrealm*

"Piccirilli is an author who knows how to terrify."
—Jack Ketchum, author of *Red*

MORE RAVES FOR TOM PICCIRILLI!

"Tom Piccirilli brings the scares home and will have you jumping at things that go bump in the night. To read a Piccirilli novel is to become a fan."

—Fearsmag.com

"Piccirilli doesn't write with ink. He writes with blood and fire, his words burning across the page and into your mind."

—*Frightmares*

"Tom Piccirilli never backs away from a disturbing or disgusting scene in the dubious interest of self-censorship, but neither does he seem to relish it as some perverted writers do (guilty, guilty, guilty). He faces it and follows it through to the consequences, and that requires bravery."

—Poppy Z. Brite, author of *Lost Souls*

"What's most fascinating about Piccirilli's work is how successfully he has translated a true sense of the Gothic into very contemporary settings."

—*The Magazine of Fantasy & Science Fiction*

"Better start revising your favorite author list—Piccirilli deserves to be at the top."

—BookLovers

AN OMEN OF DEATH

Blood spattered the snow, speckling the white.
Someone's dead.

He finally got to his own dorm, legs throbbing and weak and feeling horribly twisted, but no worse off than the inside of his own head. Even through the explosion of noise he'd made rushing into the building, slamming the heavy door behind him and huffing for breath, bleeding all over the place, the girl sitting at the security desk didn't look up. She was reading Stephen King's *Bag of Bones* and listening to Bauhaus's "Bela Lugosi's Dead" in her Walkman so loudly that the music spilled from her headphones. Cal wanted to scream but she only would have ignored him.

He skirted the empty lounge and took off toward his room, fumbling for the key, hands and coat now sticky with his drying blood. His scalp tightened as sweat trickled down his sideburns and hail melted in his hair. Bloody palm prints were all over the place.

The keys fell through his hand. A wave of dizziness shook him, and he held his breath to keep from vomiting.

As he bent to retrieve them, leaning against the knob, the door opened. . . .

NIGHT
THE
CLASS

TOM PICCIRILLI

LEISURE BOOKS NEW YORK CITY

A LEISURE BOOK®

November 2002

Published by

Dorchester Publishing Co., Inc.
276 Fifth Avenue
New York, NY 10001

ISBN 0-8439-5125-7

Visit us on the web at www.dorchesterpub.com.

To Michelle, the girl in the front row

And for Vince Harper, fellow student

I'd like to thank the following for their friendship and continuous encouragement over the years: Ed Gorman, Lee Seymour, Dallas Mayr, Douglas Clegg, Gerard Houarner, Jack Cady, Don D'Auria, and Matt Schwartz.

THE NIGHT CLASS

We are creatures of a day.
What is one, what is one not?
Man is the dream of a shadow.
                    —Pindar
                    Pythian Odes

Part One

Creatures of a Day

Chapter One

Cal's ethics class was enough to drive him to murder.

Professor Yokver ranted in front of his mahogany desk, leaping around the aisles like a lunatic minister preaching judgment and hellfire, just waiting for the speaking in tongues to take him over. He threw up his pipe-cleaner arms and gestured wildly, fingers waving like tendrils as he chanted, "What is evil, children? What is good, what is evil? Do you know?" He bashed erasers against the blackboard for emphasis, and everyone else in the class actually seemed to be enjoying the show. "Do you know, children? Do you?"

A freshman in the first row scribbled notes so

quickly he looked like a Boy Scout trying to make a campfire by rubbing two sticks together. Intent on recording every word of Yokver's tirade, the kid's tongue hung panting from his mouth. What could he possibly be writing?

Cal looked at his own empty pages.

It was a good question, though, and he wondered if he had the answer.

On the other side of the room sat Candida Celeste, smiling that say-cheese, sensuous leer that still made his entrails buck when he wasn't ready for it, showing off those perfect teeth. They made him squint, and he couldn't stare at her lips straight-on without groaning. She kept primping night-sky black hair, her cheerleader sweater opened to the fourth button—the way she'd done it back in freshman year—and dragged a pink fingernail down the length of her perfectly tanned cleavage. His first thought was that she must've gone to Florida over the Christmas vacation. And then, with sudden awful clarity, he realized, *Oh, hell, the Yok's actually turning her on.* Cal felt a painful twinge behind his eyes, this scene so surreal in its own way.

He coughed, shook his head, and checked his watch. 8:15 A.M. Another hour and twenty minutes of doom in the morning.

"Are we keeping you from some appointment of great importance, Mis-tah Prentiss?" Professor Yokver asked, wheeling in mid-stride, pacing down the aisle, up the aisle, down the aisle. The Yok knew how to throw in this funky Southern drawl when he wanted to, playing into the juice of a Flannery O'Connor character, or maybe a Georgia Peach from Carson McCullers.

At last, he stood before Cal's seat and bent to examine him with a humorless smirk.

Glancing to the left, Cal gave the professor the slow once-over as they watched each other, nearly chin to chin. Up close he saw the polka-dotted tie hanging askew, the finely trimmed goatee slightly off center and pointing at an odd slant, long hair tied into a ponytail that trailed to mid-spine. Chalk dust clung to him like mist. His spindly arms flailed so fiercely that he knocked his own glasses off, made a wheeling save, and caught them before they hit the floor. It was a nice move, actually, like the kung fu guys who toss the knives and catch them spinning as they come down, and Cal was sort of impressed.

"Please, don't let us stop you, Mr. Prentiss. Huhhh. Hessssss." Yokver hissed against the lenses of his glasses and wiped them on his lapels. The swank patterns in the hipster sports jacket entranced Cal for a moment as he tried heading into the swirls. You could ease yourself

down into them, diving deeper, and never surface again. "And where were you, hmmm?
What reverie snared you away from us, eh?"

An oncoming migraine set a tightening pair
of pincers that took a mean hold. Early morning
rush of red sunlight streamed in and caught Cal
directly across his face, brighter than Candida
Celeste's smile, the venetian blinds open just
wide enough to nail him. He winced and reared
his head back out of the glare.

Everyone turned in their seats and stared at
him. It got like this sometimes. What were they
all checking out? . . . as if someone was going
to stand and point a finger and shout,
"J'accuse!" It was easy to get a complex in a
place like this, and he felt himself heading in
that direction. The freshman in the first row
overtook his burning notes, slowed his incessant writing, and finally stopped. The kid now
swiveled in his chair and looked too.

Candida Celeste chuckled when the Yok repeated his, "Hmmm?" and so did the neckless
football player sitting diagonally from her trying his damnedest to play footsies from that angle. He wasn't going to make it, straining so
hard that Cal heard the guy's ankles pop. A couple of the others picked up on that "Hmmm" as
well, echoing the tone and swinging into it.
Willy and Rose added even more exaggerated

The Night Class

"Hmmmms?" of their own, Willy swaying in his seat, doing a little Stevie Wonder. They kept it up until they were in tune, key of F flat. Cal almost grinned. The girl seated directly in front of Candida Celeste made eye contact with him and smiled. It took a couple of seconds, but then she winked, startling the shit out of him.

"Eh, Mr. Prentiss? Where are you?"

"Right here in my seat," Cal answered.

"Not true."

"S'trewth."

"Not so."

"Okay, I'm not here at all." Maybe it was true. Sometimes it seemed to be. Anyway, the Yok liked droll answers, so let him chew on that one for a while. All Cal wanted to do now was get up and bolt. The paranoia came on pretty damn strong for this early in the morning, his high blood pressure—160 over 90 at twenty-two— jackhammering in his wrists, other thoughts caterwauling beneath the moment. The bottoms of his feet felt way too slick, as if the tile floor had been freshly waxed, and you'd take a header if you got up too quickly and tried to run.

Yokver liked to frolic in your nerve clusters. Cal said, "I'm nowhere," and tried to let it go at that, knowing, a part of him even hoping, it wouldn't be so easy.

7

"Hmm, Hhh-mmh-hhhmmm hmmm hhmm ammm," Willy and Rose went, bonding in laughter, gazing lovingly at each other even though they had no idea what they were really doing.

"Eh?" Candida said, those incisors so white and lovely.

Yok gaped, eyes filled with pride, a sorrow of some kind in there, but also a rich gratitude and appreciation for the focus. Cal knew that Yokver liked picking on him because it drew the rest of the class together. Perhaps they'd find out what was good, and what was evil, right here and now.

Cal swallowed, searching for saliva and finding only grit and moss on the roof of his mouth. "Sorry," he said, doing his best to sound sincere. Could that really be the end of it? . . . could he shimmy off the hook? It was an okay effort, but that probably wasn't going to cut it.

Yokver didn't go away.

Like a wooden clack puppet, the professor flapped around the chair with arms akimbo. He had real rhythm and athletic grace. "I didn't quite catch that, Mr. Prentiss. Did you say you were sorry?" He'd dropped the drawl, and didn't sound half as pleasing without the Dixie lilt. "And what are you sorry for?"

Plenty, Cal thought, concentrating on the

middle dots of the Yok's tie. There was a stain there. Cal sniffed. Garlic. Shrimp scampi sauce? He glanced up and saw that Yokver was actually waiting for an answer. What was the point of this kind of a drag-out? Why keep on pushing even after you'd shoved somebody up against the wall? For the theater of it? To impress the Boy Scout, to bag Candida? Could be, but probably not. Those reasons were too identifiable, too human.

Cal already knew that his one other class of the day, *The Art of Romantic Poetry in the Modern Age*, had been canceled. He just wanted to get some scrambled eggs with extra bacon at the diner, go back to his room, get a few more hours of sleep, maybe drink a six-pack later on this afternoon. He could flop for the rest of the day, do laundry, tool around on eBay for a while, and finish reading a novel he'd borrowed from Willy.

He'd wait for the night before daring to slip into the library basement and getting some real work done.

Clearing his throat, Cal made the effort to grin but couldn't get his lips to skid the right way. "Sorry for becoming distracted in the middle of your lecture. I wasn't anywhere special at this particular instant, Professor Yokver, sir." That should have been more than enough, really, Jesus. But sometimes he just couldn't stop. The cloying need in him started rising, an urgency to press back some. He couldn't tell if he was breathing anymore and really hoped he hadn't begun to pant. "Maybe I was fondly recollecting the pleasures and safety of the womb."

The Yok held his pale hands over his head, those long pale bony fingers going on and on and on, and said, "Pshaw, young master. Don't be sorry."

Cal nodded. "I'm not, really."

"No?"

"No."

He heard Jodi gasp in the seat behind him, one of those peevish, oh-please-don't-get-us-into-even-greater-misfortunes sighs. She had them down cold. She knew better than anyone how he dreaded this course, but she still expected so much out of him while he was here, and he didn't exactly understand why. Jo was the reason he'd taken Yokver's PHILO 138 class in the first place. An 8:00 A.M. meeting usually proved to be more than enough to scare him off, but they spent so little time together lately that he signed up for it at pre-registration anyway. The timing also made it more convenient to sleep over in her room, although that hadn't been playing out quite the way he thought it would, either.

The Night Class

The chummy light that danced in Yokver's eyes last week when Cal dropped the withdrawal slip on the professor's desk showed just how big a kick the Yok got out of him, now that he knew Cal hated being in here. The air had gotten so frosty that Cal thought he had seen his breath. Crumpling the slip silently, Professor Yokver dumped it into his waste basket and went back to crossing out large sections of Nietzsche's *Twilight of the Idols*.

Ten days ago Yokver had lectured that there was no such thing as motion—using an arrow as an example, saying that at each interval of time the arrow was stationary, solidified within the space it occupied at that precise instant. It was the kind of capricious rationale that could open kids' minds so long as they'd never taken physics. He drove the point home by doing cartwheels across the front of the classroom, shouting, "I am not moving!" That sounded fun when you told it, but being there threw a different, ugly spin on everything.

Later, Cal told the dean, who had doctorates in physics and chemistry as well as theology, the entire situation. Cal begged him to over-rule the drop-add forms and set him free. But the dean only gave him a lingering glare that told him he should know better than to involve the man in something like this.

11

Catch the Yok's good side as he smiled and waggled his eyebrows now, putting on a whole floor show, doing some vaudeville. "You're not sorry, eh? No, of course you're not. Then why . . . ?"

Hey, everybody had their breaking point. So just quit tearing at—

". . . did you say . . ."

—my scabs—

". . . that you were . . ."

—damn you.

". . . Calvin?"

Okay, so there they were. It was the wormy, depreciating accent Yokver put on *Calvin* that did it; the same way a bully taunted you by singing your full name while holding your lunchbox out of reach. By jabbing you in the chest, just under your heart, until the bone hurt. His name was Caleb, not Calvin, so the cheap shot failed anyway. But that wasn't the point. Were things really this out of control? Was the Yok waging a serious head game, or was it just his cholesterol getting to him again?

Cal's breath came in bites. "I thought it would be a polite way to get you off my back." He closed his empty notebook. He sort of looked forward to receiving a failing grade now. Anything to get the hell out of here.

Removing his glasses with one grand gesticulation, like Clark Kent snatching them off in an hour of need—the river flooding out the train trestle, the school bus without brakes careening on a curving mountain road—just short of yanking wide his shirt to reveal blue spandex, Yokver massaged the bridge of his nose and rubbed the indentation between his eyes frantically. His ponytail wagged over his left shoulder, then his right, as he shook his head and loudly *tsk-tsked*. "You apparently think you've got all the answers and therefore don't need to deal with the true substance of this course. So, Calvin, why don't you tell me what's really on your mind?"

Caleb smiled, and the Yok's eyebrows dropped a notch. It felt much better to be smiling. Something liquid and boiling inside suddenly became solid. His pulse was no longer thrashing around inside his wrists, but his hands still hurt a bit. He brushed his hair off his forehead and said, "If I wanted to watch a clown I'd have gone to the circus."

"Is that so?"

"It is. For a lousy ten bucks fifty midgets will come out of a Volkswagen and I can even buy one of those neon baby flashlights to spin in the dark. Even those dancing poodles are more fun than watching you cartwheel."

Jodi snorted a bothered, "Uyh, Cal." A few of

the other kids aahed and hmmed like a choir warming up. Did they think they were in grade school or sitting in church? . . . Did they want to see someone get decked, were they really that bored? Of course they were, everybody always was.

"I think the socially acceptable term currently being used is 'little people.' "

"I've been in this class for three weeks, and so far you haven't taken a second from your Atlantic City lounge act to address any ethical, moral, or social dilemmas, nor such involved issues as the afterlife, racism, censorship, pornography, abortion, or . . ." He searched for something relevant, and everything came together in one long flash of images, even though he hardly ever thought of any of it himself. ". . . prostitution, jihads, incest, Ruby Ridge, hedonism, war, or those pea brains who want to toss AIDS victims behind a fence in the desert, the new welfare laws, Social Security, Oklahoma City." He swallowed, and his spit was thicker than syrup. "Suicide."

"Oh."

Other pictures came, but he'd already run the gamut, seeing his sister again in his mind, the red washing up her arms as she reached for him. "You squash Nietzsche, insult Camus, belittle Sartre, and . . ." The Yok flicked his tongue, giving him a helpful hint. ". . . and flick your tongue at Bertrand Russell and Socrates." Cal knew he had to go for one final twist. C'mon already, the kidneys are soft tissue. "And I've caught you looking at my girl's cleavage."

Jodi grunted as if she'd been knifed, and Yokver glanced at her, focusing on her chest, that smile swinging up way higher than it should, until the corners of his mouth nearly touched his earlobes. Cal wondered when he'd let it go.

Neckless asked Candida, "Who's jihad?" She shrugged and gave Cal a sharp look that had something encouraging, frenzied, and carnal in it.

Professor Yokver snickered, mimed panic by pulling his hair, mouth wide, then waved on for more, *Bring it on home, Calvin*. There was too much blood in his face, and there was a flame somewhere inside his cloudy eyes. Caleb knew the furrow that bisected his own forehead had grown dark and deep. "But more than that, you wouldn't let me withdraw when I wanted to, you son of a bitch, and I'm not squandering any more of my life in this hell."

"No?" the Yok asked. "You've got a better hell waiting, have you?"

"Probably." Cal pointed. "And there's chalk on your tie. I'm bugging out of here. Have a nice day, everybody."

He grabbed his coat and was out the door and down two flights of steps before the crimson tinge left his vision and the full measure of what he'd done set in. Jodi might have to take the brunt of it now. He might be expelled, so that he couldn't complete the final piece of work that needed to be finished.

His mouth hurt from the tightness of the snarl he'd been holding back, the ridge of his nose ached. Sweating in the hall, he glanced at the faces of other professors as they lectured with their doors open, echoing voices snapping down the corridors of history, all of them seeming to make sense. The acoustics were good, and their words echoed and resonated in his sternum. He calmed down a little and walked outside, feeling the cold of the morning hitting hard, the February breeze tickling his hackles. He had to force his brow to un-furrow, caught up in a wave of different anger and disappointment because Jo hadn't followed him.

Caleb listened to the clock tower chime once, indicating the half hour.

8:30.

16

He'd been alive today for only forty-five minutes.

Ethics.

Jesus, God. Ethics would be the death of him.

Chapter Two

A sentence from a psychology text about Chinese Water Torture came to mind: *Seated in a comfortable chair the victim's heart would explode with the apprehension of another falling drop.*

Not very clinical when you thought about it, but there it was. Back in the lounge at his dorm, Cal dove onto the couch and tried to watch the morning news. The vertical hold was still busted from when Rocky the security guard had body-slammed a local marijuana dealer over the television, and the picture slowly skipped every few seconds. Caleb caught himself anticipating each new roll of the screen, his knees trembling like a sprinter ready to come out of the blocks. His breath writhed in his sinuses.

"Oh, boy," he murmured, pulling a frayed throw pillow into his lap. "Our head really is a snake pit this morning, isn't it?" Time crept along sideways, like a centipede slinking across his neck. This was turning out to be some day already.

The sports announcer finished showing re-runs of the plays of the week. "Now we move on to our own lovely Mary Grissom for our Accu-weather report." Capped teeth flashed. Mary Grissom flattened her pleated skirt against her thighs and held a hand up to the weather map. "Thanks, Phil. Okay, everybody, keep in mind I'm only the messenger. It'll be rough for the rest of today and tomorrow, folks, with snowfall changing to freezing rain before midnight tomorrow. . . ." Bisected by the tee-tering line that sluggishly rolled over her like a devoted lover, she continued pointing to the curving blue arrows of the coming cold front.

Hauling the pillow over his face, Cal tried to listen. By now, the rest of the dorm had begun stirring for breakfast and 9:30 classes. Hair dry-ers, showers, flushing toilets, and stereos tuned in to the university radio station KLAP drowned out the TV. His plans to take Jodi to the winter carnival tonight looked shot down in mid-flight. They couldn't catch a break lately.

"Yippie, yappie, yahoo-ooey," he muttered. "This may put the stranglehold on an already friction-filled love life."

A couple of girls from the third floor came in, hitting him with ruefully cute grins. All right, so he'd been talking to himself again. It was part of his charm. Sometimes it got that way.

"Alzheimer's, ladies," he explained. "Sets in right about the time your senior thesis is due."

With wool robes and fuzzy slippers plodding along they laughed at him, changed the channel, sat, and started watching "The Brady Bunch," neither of them irritated with the rotating picture yet. From the opening seconds Caleb could tell this was the episode where Cindy loses Kitty Carry-All—her doll that looked amazingly like "Family Affair's" Mrs. Beasley without the granny glasses, which young Buffy obsessively carried about the waist. He couldn't remember Buffy's, the actress's, real name. The brother, Johnny Whittaker, did *Tom Sawyer* and *Sigmund and the Sea Monsters*, then went and joined the Peace Corps to escape the child actor curse.

Buffy killed herself with a drug overdose, Cal remembered.

On occasion you couldn't think of anything good no matter which way you turned, not even while watching "The Brady Bunch." In the hallway, the radiator clanked with rushing water, windows above running with condensation. He stared out at the frost-covered bushes.

In class he could think of nothing he'd rather do than lie around the entire day, but now he didn't feel like reading or sleeping or doing the laundry, which really needed to be done. Packs of students marched up the hill toward the biology and physics buildings, others crossing the lawns to the humanities departments in Camden Hall, or over to the gym. He never understood how anybody could work out first thing in the morning, even though Willy often did. A telephone rang somewhere nearby.

Maybe he should go over and talk to Fruggy Fred? . . . Cal checked his watch, the crystal steamed by his sweat.

He needn't have bothered. No chance Fruggy was up at this hour. No way to be sure he'd be awake at any hour. The guy could sleep sixteen hours a day and nap a few more—he called it dream therapy and treated the subject solemnly, with reverence. Caleb often got that heavy corkscrew feeling working through his chest when Fruggy talked about it.

"If you control the dream of the world then you control the world," Fruggy Fred once drowsily said over the airwaves of KLAP, before he'd passed out at the control panel. The Doors' sullen "When the Music's Over" had played four times uninterrupted until Rocks and the other security guards battered the fire doors down.

Fruggy was out of the scene until at least three in the afternoon, when his radio shift started.

9:05.

9:06.

Caleb thought about waiting for Jodi and trying to talk her out of attending her remaining classes but knew he wouldn't be able to do it. She'd always taken grades seriously—way too intensely—even in elementary school, getting written about in her local papers for never having missed a day of grade school right up to her graduation. He understood the reason but simply wished it didn't have to be that way. He felt on the verge of becoming very whiny right now.

She believed she had to be single-minded if she wanted a chance to elude the white trash poverty that consumed the rest of her family. Two brothers and two sisters, all younger than her, already with swelling families of their own—kids they couldn't support, rap sheets for hooking, dealing, shooting dogs, a couple of retarded babies in there who'd never get the special attention they needed.

Her brother Johnny had been stabbed on six

different occasions and shot twice, and the guy still was on the street stealing cars, even with half his small intestine gone. Russell was a second-story man and liked to shimmy up drainpipes and climb trellises at night while families were eating dinner and watching sit-coms. He'd been busted five or six times already, but the police couldn't put him away for long because he never stole anything worth more than fifty bucks. Mostly change jugs, women's shoes, clock radios, old black-and-white photographs, and any *Reader's Digests* that might be lying around. He wasn't really a burglar, Caleb knew, but some kind of fetishist.

Cal also had a bad feeling that her brothers might have sexually abused her at some point, with their brown teeth and pork bellies and tattoos stirring up a significantly lurid mental picture, although she never said as much. Jo occasionally kicked and wept while dreaming. Caleb wondered if he could set Fruggy Fred after her during a nightmare, tell him to go in and hunt around her subconscious and come back with the whole truth.

It proved particularly incongruent that her alcoholic mother still kept the scrapbooks of Jodi's first attempts at handwriting and math, with gold stars and smiley faces pasted all over everything. He'd flipped through the collection of papers, page after page where even the tiniest kindergarten print was perfect. Each project flawlessly done: the digestive tract drawn in precise scale, the limbic system, weather maps more detailed than Mary Grissom's, every paper thorough and accomplished, going back year after year. What five-year-old never got her *b*s and *d*s mixed up?

Now in the last semester of their senior year, she'd grown even more absorbed in her studies. So much between them, unsaid and inferred, with even more burgeoning every day. She had to go to the dentist to get a hard plastic night-guard because she'd started grinding her back teeth so badly. The official term was bruxism, and the noise kept him up at night and distracted the hell out of him during the day. She couldn't even hear it anymore, it had become so much a part of her.

Her grade point average, letters of reference, contacts among the faculty, and her research paper: *Schizophrenia as Stimuli and a Means to the Expression of Racial Memory, Primal Fear, and the Ascension of the Human Animal Mind.* He had no clue what it meant, or what was involved in its meaning. She'd tried to explain it to him once but they'd made love instead. It was the much better deal.

9:10.

Caleb rested his forearms against the window, observing the present before it could slip even further away. Next year Jo would be in medical school, and as much as she promised that it wouldn't affect their relationship, she couldn't keep the truth out of her eyes. It was already unraveling. He hoped his own lies weren't so obvious but had a feeling they were.

That telephone up the corridor continued to ring, finally rousing him. He drifted, wondering if anyone would answer it. The radiator rumbled off. On about the fortieth ring, he realized it was his own phone.

He pulled out his key as he rushed down the hall, almost but not really sure that whoever had hung on this long would probably wait another minute. Wearing only his socks he slid on the tile floor and almost took a header into the wall. On the run he reached his room, fit the key in the lock, and turned the knob. Who wanted him this badly?

In one slithery motion the door opened much more easily than it should have, knob whipping out of his hand, and his momentum carried him inside too fast. Skidding on the throw rug, he kept his balance but nearly went head over knees as he knocked aside the desk chair. Christ, he was going to break a leg this way. Books launched off his shelf and the peanut butter jar atop the cube refrigerator fell and shattered.

"Damn." He snatched the phone out of the cradle. "Hello?" He carefully nudged the larger pieces of glass into a pile with the side of his foot. "Anyone there? Hey, don't give up on me now. I'm here."

No dial tone, and no static from a bad connection.

Dead air waited, so frigid that he could almost feel a drop in temperature.

"Hel . . . ?"

Emptiness. Waiting, the dry silence went on unchanging for another five heartbeats, now eight, ten, as he counted them without reason. No breathing on the other end that he could hear, no train whistles or background sound at all to give him a sign. No suggestion of humanity, and that's why he held on for so long, because it had waited so long for him.

As he leaned farther into the receiver he thought he could sense a presence. Something much larger than himself was trying to draw him in. He hesitated to say anything else—the heavy hush so pervasive it felt like there was no phone in his hand, no ear to listen to it.

Seventeen, nineteen, twenty-five heartbeats, and this was getting ridiculous, he understood that, but there were these frissons working his spine now, his underarms heavy with goose-flesh. This wasn't a wrong number; somebody wanted him desperately. *Who the hell is this and why won't you talk to me?*

Finally, as he opened his mouth to utter something, he had no idea what, a sound like crunching ice crackled sharply in his ear. Crumpling plastic? Somebody chewing? It fell away to a droning buzz, followed by a high-pitched squeal of distant laughter or sirens or stuck pigs or feedback, and he jerked the receiver away with a groan. Jagged noises afterwards, brittle coughs and dry leaves breaking off piece by piece over the line.

He held the phone an inch away from his ear. A faint and faraway voice rustled unintelligibly.

"Is . . . anyone there?" Something rigid started to loosen up and swirl around inside his chest. "Hey!" he shouted. "Come on, c'mon. Speak up."

Another ethereal whimper, clearer now but not distinct, still so removed that the edge of his ears burned as he strained, trying to drive himself down into the phone, reaching for the words.

Ghosts wanted him dead.

"Who is this?" he whispered back, thinking how his door had glided open too easily, and knowing that someone else had been inside his

27

room and had left without locking up.

Cal threw the phone across the room. It broke against the wall where the bloodstains jabbed through a thin layer of peach paint.

Chapter Three

He had to take a chance and drop into the library basement in daylight.

Not that anyone would notice, and if they did, who'd care about seeing a guy lurking behind a veil of branches and slipping through a mud-smeared window with a broken latch? What was he going to steal—*The Collected Works of George Eliot*? *Les Fleurs du Mal*? How about a copy of Donald Barthelme's *The Dead Father* or *Snow White*? So far as sneakiness was concerned, breaking into the library didn't rate high on the scale.

But if you were around last year at about four in the morning at the end of March, and were awakened by awful panting and unknown

29

noises heading up toward your second-floor window, and you happened to get out of bed and draw back your blinds to take a look—having dreamed of your sister again, reaching for you with red arms—only to yell and hop a foot in the air when you saw this humongous milk-white ass shining at you in the moonlight, all 340 pounds of Fruggy Fred playing Human Fly on the wall, extremely agile actually, for a guy his size, keeping all his weight on his toes and hanging on to the brick like a rock climber, naked and smeared with something slick and glistening, maybe baby oil or Vaseline or maple syrup or even honey, silently scaling the wall covered with thick ivy in order to get back into the locked dorm, only minutes after having run from his girlfriend's room, making the grand escape during a vicious fight with the butter knife–wielding lady because he'd fouled the final moments of romantic milieu just before making love, having fallen asleep in the middle of foreplay again . . . hey, now *that* was an attempt at some seriously surreptitious movement.

Sneaking into the library didn't even count, really, but Cal still didn't like the idea of going into the basement during the morning. Nervous pressure knotted his shoulders. This venture hooked into his imagination. He had started thinking about his sister again, and that was never a good sign. He glanced at his hands but kept moving. A subtle but intense sense of fear stung his midriff as he left the dorm and crossed the wide back lawn. Frigid February air cooled his face.

He couldn't quite figure out how he'd started this affair with a dead stranger or where he expected it to take him.

The more he hoped to put circumstances into words, the increasingly morbid his thoughts became. You knew it was getting pretty bad when you even noticed it yourself. Caleb always tried to be wary about slipping too far over the side, wondering about the predisposition in his genetic makeup. Was that inside him? The need to crawl into the bathtub with something sharp?

Walking the path as the sky roiled like white gauze tearing, he thought, *They lock people like you in the wards and rubber rooms.*

Adding, after a time, *Yeah, they do, but they always let us out again.*

If Jodi had known about his thesis she would have slapped him with a string of appalling psychological names and phrases—Obsessional Neuroses of Spatial Taboos, Anxiety-Hysteria Polarity, Ego and Urination in Dream States, Free-floating Castration Cathexis—or worse.

She'd make him the star subject for one of her abnormal psych papers. She'd start interviewing him on tape, and make him look at ink blots shaped like the asses of teenage girls. They'd get some notice, do a run on local cable television, the morning shows, and then take it on the road. He could tour the country in a cage while she wore a top hat and held a lion tamer's whip, and after the show he'd lie in the corner on top of a pile of hay and try to get kids to throw him unshelled peanuts.

Clearly, he'd gone too far to quit. The thesis had grown into a book, and the book had taken on a bizarre afterlife of its own. That musty room hidden in the twisting dark bowels of the library's storage basement tunnels had become a part of him, and so had the girl.

The breeze blew harder, and Cal pressed his hands deeper into his pockets, grabbing fistfuls of torn lining and his folded notes and papers. The clock tower chimed once.

9:30.

Sylvia Campbell was dead at the age of eighteen.

Murdered six weeks ago during the winter intercession, in Caleb's room, under the window where she'd moved his bed, probably so she could sleep comfortably without the heat of the radiator keeping her awake. Caleb didn't mind the hot air on him all night long, but for some reason he'd left the bed where she'd put it.

Who were you?

For convenience sake the university left only two dormitories open full-time during the intercession, enough to house the 400 students who took the winter courses offered during the five interim weeks between the fall and spring semesters. Cal had been thinking of quitting school or switching dorms or doing some damn thing to face off against the world. He moved out and placed his possessions in a storage closet, wondering if he'd ever be back: all the stuff he wasn't taking with him over the Christmas vacation break.

In four years he'd never had the same room twice—it was part of what he needed to make him feel like he was actually doing something with his life already—but in his last semester they'd allowed him to keep this one. He didn't want it, but they'd never bothered to assign him another. The intercession placement program would allocate a different student to his room for the length of the session. It sounded like a lot of trouble, but he never thought about it too much.

Why did you lie?

The day before Christmas Eve, about an hour after his last final, he'd kissed Jodi good-bye and taken off, telling her he would be staying with a high school friend in Montana for the vacation. He had no high school friends, in Montana or anywhere else, but he didn't want her to pity him the fact, and worse, certainly didn't want to spend a month with her family. He left with the idea of wandering the country a la Kerouac, maybe, doing some damn thing, and hoping not to run into any serial killers out there. He thought he might still be filled with adolescent enthusiasm and aspirations left over from puberty; it seemed he would never get over it.

Hitching along interstate highways, he learned that even truck drivers of the day were reluctant to pick up hitchhikers. Cal didn't blame them. He eventually wound up renting a Mazda and scurrying past all the places he thought might've looked interesting. Somehow he'd gotten trashed out on the West Coast for two weeks when he'd planned on visiting New England. The Mazda broke down in Arizona and he found himself in the back of a pickup with about fifteen Navajos. They let him off in a town called Blue that was maybe fifty yards long. He didn't know what the hell he was doing.

His binge drinking had started when he was fifteen, but he'd been sober for a couple of years, or thought he'd been. He couldn't recall even taking a pull, but his breath smelled like rum all the time now.

The silky embrace of failure had found him again and was laughing loudly: through the scrub grass it hid in wait behind the Ma-and-Pa grotesqueries and cactus tourist attractions, riding the cripple-winged foals and two-headed calves. It took him another week to hit the California beaches, and his sweat stank like mash whiskey. Writing when he wasn't too weak and sunburned to find the keys of his laptop, most of his disks had already melted. His hair had been bleached to a dull shade of sand.

He woke up in the middle of January with two sprained knees and shards from a busted bottle of 151 Rum embedded in his hands after a fall down an embankment outside Sparks, Nevada, that left him in traction for three days. The nurses ignored him and the doctors treated him with a careless disregard, almost nobody bothering to say a word to him no matter what he asked. Most of the journey he couldn't remember, and what he could he wanted to forget.

The long haul ended with Caleb on crutches, bandaged and limping up to Jodi's dilapidated front porch. Her brother Russell was flipping through black-and-white photos, chuckling to himself. Johnny had four stolen Toyotas parked side by side at the edge of the woods where he was painting them all lemon yellow with a brush and a bucket. The retarded babies crawled and mewled in the yard; her belligerent father and drunk mother threatening to shake shotguns in Cal's face. He liked the attention. Eventually they let him camp in the backyard where he baby-sat a hydrocephalic kid every afternoon. Jo didn't ask too many questions. In its own fashion, that had been the best and worst part of it all.

Nearly healed—so far as his legs were concerned—he returned to school to discover his walls had been freshly coated a ratty peach that didn't do anything to conceal the fact that someone in the corner of his room had died very badly. The place smelled like the crusty scabs in his hands even with the windows wide open and the room freezing, giving it a meat locker feel.

As he'd gazed at the stains, Willy had come in to ask about his trip to New England. He could only stare at the wall.

In a way, he was still staring at it.

Caleb turned his face into the gnawing wind as he came out of the field.

9:43.

Torn wads of pocket lining filled each of his sweating hands. Jodi would be crushed when she found out the carnival would be shut down tonight due to the snow—she'd been talking about it for the past week, filled with an almost giddy whimsy he'd rarely seen in her. It sort of scared him. Perhaps what had attracted him in the first place was that overly serious side of her, giving him something to latch on to when he needed to balance out.

It was a relief to discover their gentle rapport was still there though, sometimes, and that he didn't always have to love her against the tide of their inevitable parting.

"Win me a stuffed animal?" she'd asked yesterday.

What else could you say except, *Sure, of course.* He'd never won a stuffed animal for a girl before and couldn't get over it, thinking, *How could I have forgotten to do something like that?* Every guy should win a pretty girl a toy at the carnival at least once in his life. He'd have to do it. Knock over the cans, toss the rings, float the Ping-Pong ball, and win the pink elephant. He just hoped that wasn't the same way her father had met her mother.

Caleb jogged down a sharp slope that swept into a gully and came to a crumbling cobbled path at the north side of the library. Grabbing hold of the chain-link fence surrounding the back of the building, he hefted himself up. Cold metal seared his palms.

If you walked in the front door on the other side of the library, you'd have to pass through the security system turnstile before you got to the book checkout counters, microfiche machines, and reference desks on the first floor. The basement doors, three of them, were kept locked.

Because the library and student union were interconnected by a transverse bridge, built into the side of a steeply inclined hill, Cal was already below ground level back here. Several dorms were erected in the same fashion, the campus filled with promontories and gradients, copses and meadows fairly wild in some areas. The lush countryside was a main selling point in the school brochures.

Climbing, he watched the students passing before the windows above him. At the top of the fence he swung his legs over, ready to leap down, but in the middle of vaulting his coat snagged a barb and he was thrown off-kilter. He briefly wondered if maybe he'd been drinking again without realizing it. Spinning, he heard something rip, and the worst of his two bad knees painfully cracked sideways. He yelped and came down on a mound of frozen earth.

"Hey!" someone shouted.

With his heart bucking, Cal felt like an idiot for the complete lack of coiled-muscle, cougar-like agility he'd just displayed. Jesus Christ, Fruggy Fred climbed three floors of an entire dorm covered in vegetable oil and never lost a toehold. Maybe he should give lessons, start Cal off smothered in margarine, showing him how to shift his weight, plant his feet just the right way.

"Hey!"

Goddamn, what was going on now? He felt the soft touch of the dead coming for him again. He snorted like a horse, angrily, trying not to bite through his tongue. Caleb's imagination hadn't let up for the last half hour, and he thought for sure the CIA, Mossad, or the seven angels from Revelations had gotten the drop on him as he heard the voice calling.

Veering, Cal saw the girl who'd winked at him in his ethics class this morning leaning casually against the fence. "Hey," she said, pulling a grimace. "You okay? That looked like it might've hurt."

"Yeah," he told her. "Sure. I'm fine."

She stuck her fingers through the chain link and wriggled them at him.

Dark hair bobbed around her cheeks to frame her face perfectly. They called it a heart-shaped face in mysteries from the fifties, and he wasn't about to argue with it. She was an attractive brunette, petite, with pouty lips and large brown eyes that dominated her features. She had a beauty mark at the corner of her left eyebrow that made him notice her gaze even more. No matter where you tried to look, you were drawn right back to it. When she blinked her long lashes swiped the air with a mentally audible whip-crack. Her voice was a little rough, with some flint in it, so that you definitely knew you were being talked to.

"What are you doing over there?" she asked.

"Uhm . . ."

"That was a heck of a flip you just did," she said, and giggled deep in the back of her throat, where it counted.

"Learned everything I know from the Flying Walendas," he said, hoping he wasn't scowling. He forced his brow to straighten out, making sure he didn't squint, and added, "But not the dead ones."

"Uh-huh. Well, that's good, I suppose."

Cal was unsure of what she might read from him. "Don't tell me that class was let out early today." It would've ended only ten minutes ago. There was no way for her to get across the quad in that amount of time. "And Yokver likes to keep the show going to the very last minute."

She shrugged, and the hair flapped at the

hinges of her jaw. "Can't care about that anymore. It irritates me the way he plays to the audience like that. I walked out after you did."

That genuinely surprised him. "Really? I thought everyone else loved the Yok's class."

"I don't think any of us actually like it. He doesn't say much of anything at all." She pursed her lips, and wet them absently with her tongue until they glistened, trying to come up with an answer. It was undoubtedly the kind of move the Yok would have liked a great deal, as sensuous as Candida Celeste's pink fingernails plucking at her blouse. "It's a simplistic class and appeals to people who don't feel like thinking much before noon. Count me guilty."

"Me too." It was true.

"I guess I felt the same way you did the whole time and just never cared enough to budge. He just wants bodies in front of him, doesn't matter who they are or what they might have to add. It's a damn waste. But the system make it so hard to switch classes, and by then apathy takes hold, and you start thinking the hell with it. Easier just to sit there and zone out, figuring that you got a dog of a course." Her breath blew out in small white puffs of steam that reminded him of Snoopy's balloon thoughts. "You're lucky you didn't break your neck. You tore your coat to pieces. Just what are you doing over there?"

The beauty mark drew his stare. "I thought this might be a shortcut into the student union."

"Nope," she said. "It's a dead end. There's no back door over here. You have to go around the other way, over the hill."

"So I see now."

Cal yanked his ripped coat closed, making sure his notes were in place, and climbed back over the fence. He took his time for both ego's sake and because his knees were wracked. Landing next to her, she held up an invisible score card. "An inspired performance."

He took a bow and she clapped politely, the comedy not quite there yet although they were both trying. She had one of those smiles you couldn't help but smile back at, no matter how foul a mood you were in. That could drive you nuts if you wanted to sulk; that was real power.

He stuck out his hand. "I'm Caleb Prentiss."

With a gasp she grabbed his wrist and pulled him in too close, jutting forward until her nose touched his. What? He parted his lips for a kiss, frowning, wondering how they'd jumped all the way to this so quickly. His tongue hung loose in his mouth.

She said, " 'Calvin! Well, Mis-tah Prentiss,

now I can see what your dire urgency is about. Eh? Eh? Hmmm? Hmmmmmm?' "

He burst out laughing, more like braying, sounding strange and idiotic, but at least it was funny. She fell back against the fence chuckling, took his hand and said, "My name is Melissa Lea."

"Fine impersonation. You could be the Yok's daughter."

Brushing a black curl from her mouth, she said, "I am."

Whoa, my goodness. It stopped him hard. He gagged on nothing, and the flush of humiliation crawled along his neck. Wind blew turgid bits of air up his nose as he stammered to speak, but wait, hadn't she . . . ?

"Don't have a heart attack," Melissa Lea said. "I'm only kidding. My last name is McGowan. What's the matter? Ease up a little."

He had to try. "That was sort of a nasty trick."

"Professor Yokver has really got you spooked, huh?"

Why hadn't he seen her before today? Why didn't he recognize her? Had the Yok bent him so far out of shape? . . . was he truly that fragile when you got down to it? "I don't remember you ever saying much in class, Melissa."

"Did anybody?"

She was right. Nobody ever spoke much, not

43

even the frosh who acted like he actually cared about the ethics class. "No."

"Yeah, well, I'd heard nothing but rave reviews about him from other people, and how it was supposed to be such an 'easy' grade. That should've been the tip-off. They told me he'd been voted the most popular professor for the last six or seven years, but after the first few meetings I figured out that the exhilarating PHILO One-thirty-eight was going to drag my already crummy GPA into the gutter. By then I was stuck, and he wouldn't let me leave no matter how much I asked."

"And the dean wouldn't let you out either."

"No, he wouldn't, and I don't know why. I think that man pisses me off more than Yokver. There's something about him . . . the way he looks at people. There always seems to be something else on his mind, you know?"

"Yes."

"Like he's not even listening. It gets to me on occasion."

Cal felt it too, whenever he had to deal with the dean. They walked back toward the open field. With only the hint of a sneer, her smile drifted and became a sensual suggestion. He thought so anyway.

"So," Melissa said, "when I heard you speaking your mind during that little tête à tête this morning, it just snapped things into perspective for me, and shook me out of my complacency. I mean, to realize I'm paying for this. I've just been kind of wandering around for a while. I've been thinking of transferring and might just take the chance on going someplace else."

"Where?"

"Who knows? I'm not sure." She kept up the smile, but her face had darkened—transferring to a new university could be worse than immigrating. It would be like entering a new country where you were the outlander all over again, and needed to learn a new difficult language, a different set of rules. It kept him from going. "Now I've got to get back to my room and finish off a paper on Spenser's 'Lines on his Promised Pension' for Professor Moored."

"An English major?" he asked.

"With a Spanish minor, *comprendes?*"

"Got it. Spenser. I never liked him much."

"Me neither. Nobody does, so maybe the professor won't be stuck having nine other papers on the same subject, the way he will with 'Kubla Khan,' 'Ode on a Grecian Urn,' and 'The Raven.'"

Howard Moored was particularly fond of Shakespeare's sonnets, which nobody ever wrote about because they were all deceptively similar. Cal wanted to talk to her about it, lend her some books, give her a few insights, but now, suddenly, she seemed to be in a rush, and he felt as if he were keeping her. "Good luck with it. Nice chatting with you."

"You too, 'bye."

He watched her cross the dried grass with a quick but heavy tread, hair tugged briefly by the breeze. His Adam's apple felt larger than his head as bad ideas started circling and diving. *Ah, no, don't do it, don't even think it, you're going to get into such deep shit*, but he couldn't stop himself and there was nobody else there to knock him down.

Impossible to keep from asking—so when she was fifty yards away he shouted, "Hey, Melissa, since neither of us has a class to go to tomorrow morning, would you like to get breakfast together?"

She faced him and walked backward several steps. "Okay! We can talk about jihads, censorship, pornography, Ruby Ridge, and midgets."

"Well, yeah, I suppose we could do all that, so long as we don't touch on the subject of motion. I'll meet you in the cafeteria at eight."

She waved an all-right motion, almost a power-to-you sign.

When she'd faded from sight he reached into the pocket of his coat to make sure his notes hadn't been lost. Papers crinkled aggressively at his touch. He folded them to keep them safe and slowly worked his way over the fence again, careful of the barbs this time, and cautiously jumped down on the other side.

Moving behind the branches, he yanked the spindly tree from his face and sneaked to the dirty window. His palms were sweaty again, and he sniffed at his hands to make sure there wasn't any odor of mash whiskey coming from him.

Pressing his weight against one edge of the frame, he shoved at the hinges until the latch he'd broken a week earlier jiggled open.

From there he shifted his feet, crouched and stared into the darkness of the secluded room below, seeing clearly for the first time just how much like a tomb it truly was inside.

What do angels dream?

Chapter Four

Hopping down from the window ledge, into the shadows, he tripped over Sylvia's wicker love-seat the same way he'd stumbled onto her death in the first place.

Lying sideways in the chair, he felt the wicker braids and knots bulging beneath his back. "All right, so I'm back again," he said through clenched teeth. The milieu of the place made you whisper like this, that sense of hallowed ground all around you, atmosphere so heavy it felt like being straddled by a great, living weight. You could get caught up in symbols without even having to look hard.

He grew acutely aware that he now sat in a dead girl's chair.

Dead, as in Ted Bundy or Richard Speck catching and killing you dead, her presence growing in his mind while he became more uneasy yet exceptionally snug, realizing this was a love seat, meant for two. Again it seemed that this had been his fate for longer than he could remember. He and Sylvia together down here and trying to get to know each other a little better, a blind date of a much different kind.

Feeling his way through the blackness, he found the light switch beside the door, flicked it, and scanned the tiny room.

Perhaps not a tomb exactly. More like a coffin.

The single light bulb above lit a musty storage room stuffed with the remains of Sylvia Campbell's life: her furniture and clothes, a decrepit orange crate containing paperbacks. She had good taste in literature, and owned just about every book written by John Irving, Joyce Carol Oates, José Saramango, William S. Burroughs, Donald Barthelme, and John Fowles. Like him, she didn't go in for linear plotlines. A pink toothbrush had been shoved inside a box of envelopes, and above it sat a sheaf of loose-leaf paper, which he now used to write out his thesis in longhand.

This was all she had left behind. Maybe sixty pounds of possessions if you totaled it up. If he died tomorrow he'd have just a tad less to show for the entirety of his own life.

He took off his shredded coat and crouched among her belongings, touching them here and there, marking different textures. He envisioned her gestures, a voice and laughter, style and manner, and drew out thickly detailed scenarios, pondering what it must have been like to live with these things day in and out. These objects that had seen her die.

In the beginning of this . . . research . . . he had checked the mattress for indentations, scanning for the deeply set outlines of her and her men, trying to discriminate between those of himself and Jodi on his own bed. There weren't many bloodstains on the mattress, not as many as you might think. Plenty of scenes threw themselves at him as he tried to find her there: at eighteen there was still time enough to be a virgin, wasn't there? Maybe not.

Perhaps she'd left her boyfriend far back in some Midwestern corn crop, or had a guy on campus she preferred staying with. Cal tapped the box spring and listened to the tight metal coils' vibrating hum.

Had an angry lover decided to take her life? The kid's sitting at the desk long past midnight, poring over logarithms and implicit differentiation and hyperbolic functions, his accelerated calculus homework thrashing his ass to pieces. No matter how long he glowers at the books he's going to fail, and he knows it. His father will give him hard glares of disappointment, his mother will wring her hands on her apron and snarl at him with waxy lips. His brother the chiropractor will try to take him into the business, teach him to give massages, gently crack the atlas vertebra.

So he looks over and stares at Sylvia snuggled under the covers, sleeping so easily, not a trouble in the world. He starts thinking that he's fighting the battle for her, to get her the house she wants, to be able to afford the three children she's always talking about, the cocker spaniel and a couple of cats and the fish pond with the motorized waterwheel, a new truck to go camping in with the kids; he's doing all of this for her and she's not suffering in the slightest, just lying there breathing softly in her sleep. How can he deal with that day in and out, can't she hear him suffering here? Why doesn't she know he's shrieking?

Who were you?

The question came alive in the stillness, the one that mattered most. It grated against Caleb. There was some bitterness right from the beginning of this journey because he knew he'd never be able to entirely finish it. No matter how far he went or how much he gave. A grail always beyond his grasp, unless he too was dead.

"Shut up," he said aloud.

His voice rang around the room.

That first day back at school he'd stared at the peach paint covering the blood on the wall while Willy repeatedly asked him about his vacation. Christ, he knew somebody had died here.

He knew his sister was on her way.

Willy was a weightlifter who stood 6'5" of solid muscle, an imposing figure as he leaned over Caleb trying to grasp his friend's attention. Cal couldn't look away from the wall; he knew bloodstains when he saw them. Willy kept quizzing him about Christmas and New Year's, asking about New England lovelies, wild Ivy League times. "How badly in trouble did you get? I mean, you have that look in your eye. You got to Boston, didn't you? You must've hit the Combat Zone at some point, no? It's nothing like it used to be, they tell me, but still, you gotta go down there. Remember my old roommate, Herbie Johnson? Nah, you wouldn't; well, he came from Massachusetts, used to tell me all kinds of funky stories about the Zone before they cleaned it up. At least Disney hasn't taken it over yet like Times Square. Hey, I hear that's where they . . ."

Willy didn't notice the new color of Caleb's room, didn't seem to mind the terrible lingering smell of decomposition that tore at Cal's sinuses. The windowsill was frosted with rime.

No way to be positive about what had happened while he'd been away, but Cal stood entranced, looking at the ugly area of the wall, sniffing the meaty stench.

At that instant, he heard his dead sister's voice in his ear as clearly as though she were standing behind him.

He whirled as if a blade had been flicked against his kidneys—scared, revolted, and sick, twisting sideways to get a better look at someone who wasn't there anymore. He bit his tongue until she vanished back into his childhood, where all the ghosts—or at least most of them—had been stored. Willy kept talking, starting to look a little annoyed. Cal's palms itched as though tickled by spikes. He watched the wall, knowing the blood, understanding why his sister had come back, tying things together as the seconds counted off.

Willy grew more agitated as he repeated Cal's name, grabbed an arm and tried to rattle him loose. "Hey, you all right? What's the matter? What'd I say?"

Caleb's heartbeats grew too loud in his head as he thought, *Okay, so that's someone's blood*

*splashed on my wall, in my own room . . . who?
. . . what? . . . the bed's been moved,* and Willy
pulled harder, but Caleb wouldn't turn yet. The
fact that the red could still be seen beneath so
much peach paint proved it had coagulated and
been left there for a while. Two, three days?
They didn't find her right away, she must've
been a loner, no friends searching her out, why
didn't anyone smell it? . . . *never realizing that
he'd only assumed the victim had to be a
woman, not even considering she was a suicide.
No one would spill that much of their own blood
against a wall, not even if they shot themselves
in the mouth.* Maybe that was true. It seemed
that it would be true.

Willy had started shouting by then, drawing
his large, powerful hand back to slap Cal's face,
perhaps playfully but probably not. "Cal! What
the hell are you doing?" Rose came walking into
the room with Fruggy Fred bouncing behind
her reading a worn copy of Ursula K. Le Guin's
The Lathe of Heaven. Déjà vu slammed Caleb,
and what had been disjointed fell perfectly into
place.

Rose said, "I heard about your legs. Are you
okay? Cal? Hey, what's the matter? What's going on in here?" She hit a pose like a scared
badger, neck bent too far forward, hands hanging from her wrists like paws. "What are you

two doing?" Willy finished drawing his massive arm back and started to bring his fist down, picking up speed as it came like a hammer hurled from overhead, and Cal let go of one crutch and blocked Willy's slap. Some things you do on instinct. It jarred him anyway, though, and his teeth snapped together.

He never thought for a second that the killer had been found.

Fruggy hugged him and murmured in his ear, laid down on the bed and instantly fell asleep, the center of the mattress sinking nearly to the floor. Cal looked closer and saw that it wasn't his mattress at all; this was a brand-new one. What happened to the old one? Where did they put it?

Willy relaxed and put his arm around Cal's shoulders and said, "You must've had a hell of a fun time if you're still wigging out. You did go to the Combat Zone, right? Like I was saying, Herbie Johnson used to tell me about . . ."

Rose shut the windows and helped him unpack. "It's freezing in here. You're all sunburned. You coming to our get-together tonight?" She put his underwear away, and for some reason that made his scalp prickle. "What happened to your hands? Jodi didn't tell me about how badly you'd cut your hands. Holy shit, you need some antibiotic ointment and a bandage. Oh, Cal . . ."

"Cut them on a broken bottle of rum," Caleb answered, listening to his own voice, so far away that it sounded as if he were already out there with his sister. "No big deal, really."

"You're bleeding," Willy said.

He looked down and saw his palms spotting. "It's nothing." He tried a grin, and it felt as if his lips were breaking off. But he had to make small talk. "So, what's been going on with you two? How'd Christmas and New Year's treat you both?"

Fruggy's soft snores accented their friendship as Willy and Rose told him what they'd received and given over the holidays, what clubs they'd been to, how their families were, other classmates they'd seen and stories they'd heard, and Cal couldn't remember a damn word about any of it.

He could still smell Sylvia in the room.

Branches scraped angrily against the windows of this coffin, battered by the rising wind.

Caleb sat in Sylvia Campbell's love seat and took out his notes, straightening them and struggling to read in the dim light. His script didn't look the same and he couldn't figure out what he'd written. There were pages and pages, but he didn't know where he'd started or where he'd left off. Shadows refused to speak to him this time.

Until he'd discovered the small self-portrait pencil drawing she'd done, he hadn't known what Sylvia Campbell looked like. She'd kept no photo albums along with her belongings. Though he'd found a purse—one of those big purple plastic wrinkled things like a giant raisin—there'd been no driver's license, college ID, no address books, or even cash for that matter. The cops, or somebody, must have taken it all.

Before finding the scrap paper sketch, he'd been forced to use Jodi's features as a starting point when conjuring Sylvia. The more he thought about it, the more he realized he needed a visual image to work with as he wrote about her. Bringing Sylvia to life was necessary if he was going to feel her in his guts, and get the slow burn going. He'd smoothed a few lines around Jo's brow, lengthened and curled her blond hair, switched the color of her eyes from blue to an off-hazel, and altered the shape of her nose just a bit, giving him someone else yet retaining familiarity. You cannot create, you can only embellish.

He could love her, in a manner, as he loved Jodi, in order to grow that much closer to who she'd been, in a way that mattered. In the beginning it had been difficult to keep the new face from melting back into Jo's, but eventually his vision of Sylvia could move like a marionette through a life he attempted to string together.

It didn't always work. Sometimes the strings got tangled. At other times she became his sister, and the puppet mouth would be moving, trying to tell him something that just wasn't coming through.

The pencil drawing itself had been done on the back of an index card she'd used as a bookmark, placed at page 395 of Joyce Carol Oates's *Bellefleur*, a chapter entitled "The Wicked Son." Cal had always wanted to read the book, but he'd been intimidated by its 700 small-print pages.

He'd flipped through each of Sylvia's paperbacks and the sketch had flown free, just an index card arching onto the windowsill like a luna moth alighting. By that time he'd been having dreams about her, nightmares involving vivisection that made him breathless before dawn and gave him night terrors, until Jo sobbed in nervous fear and had to shake him awake. The plastic nightguard made it seem as if she had no teeth, just a black hole there in the center of her face where it made him want to scream. Looking up at Jodi as the sweat slid into his eyes, he'd once started to say Sylvia's name before realizing where he was.

Sylvia Campbell didn't look anything like the marionette he'd pictured, although for some vague reason he'd hoped she would. He'd erred on the side of caution anyway, because she was far more beautiful than he'd imagined. She was an altogether different woman than the chimera dragging painfully through his dreams. The sketch was signed *Sy. C.*, faintly smudged about the edges. A caption printed beneath her face read simply, *Me*.

And so there they were.

It had been a pleasant shock to finally meet her. Graceful curves and swirling graphite shading of pigments brought a reality to her that had been lacking before. He clung to the index card with an intensity that startled him, afraid to fold or bend it. He knew he was in trouble. He recognized that he was smiling too much, repeatedly tracing the outline of her eyes, holding her face in his hands. This was bad.

She wasn't self-conscious. Long black tresses twirled curling down past one eye, grinning back at him with her bottom lip out in a near pout, a pretty deep gaze catching him off guard. He could almost believe she watched him from the grave, beckoning him forward.

"Shut up," Caleb said with more resignation, trying to give it an extra kick. It didn't work. He sighed too loudly for the room and spread his notes, tapping his pen.

After Willy and Rose left him on that first day of class this semester, Fruggy Fred snored in the bed as Cal sat on the floor rubbing his legs, trying to sort the conflicting messages.

There was murder here, and nobody had even warned him. No yellow police tape over the door. No note from the dean. Fruggy turned over, and turned again, mouth moving nonstop. Cal wondered who he was having such intense conversations with. He bent to listen but couldn't make out the words. He got closer to the wall and stared at the bad paint job.

He'd smelled this before.

After she'd decided—in the last week as a novitiate before her final vows—not to go through with it and become a nun, his sister went to work as a social worker before the term became too cliché.

Back then, when you still had the spillover from Vietnam, and Amer-Asian children were coming over by the boatload looking for their fathers, and the Cubans were kept in cages in the underpasses and deported back to Castro, everybody shrieking, and the Death Squads marched up through South America and into suburbia, white-bread girls still looked at Harlem as a sort of Mecca for furthering the Black movement, and nobody knew what the hell they were doing anymore. It was all right, at least they were making an effort. Crack and AIDS hovered, descending to pluck at the fabric of the world, just waiting for the final minutes of disco to die out.

She'd gone on to describe more horrors to him than he could ever forgive her for. She hadn't meant for it to happen, for him to pick up on so much of what she'd muttered and sobbed about, but even at five he'd had a penchant for damnation.

Eventually, though, he'd forgotten most of the finer details of what she'd said, and he'd caught himself actually *trying to remember*, going after the flitting memories, and still wanting to think kindly of her.

Rat stories were some of her favorites, as she held him on her knee and he watched cartoons. Telling him how they chewed the thick meat of the thighs of infants and the homeless, where they got inside the dying and came out their throats. How she had held her hands over kids' stomachs after a liquor store holdup on Jerome Avenue had gone very bad, and about when twelve-year-old girls left their babies stopping up toilets, and how there were husbands who lit their wives on fire for overcooking hamburger. His sister said something to him about once being raped by three guys in a green van, who'd wanted to nab themselves a nun.

On a cloudy afternoon when he was seven, after she'd just quit working in the Bronx and began baby-sitting him for Mother, she sat in the bathtub as the rain came ripping down and pulsed against the windows. She slit her wrists vertically the length of her forearms—which was important if you were serious about it to keep the blood from clotting—and called him in from watching television to ask him to read passages from the Bible to her. He'd done it before, and enjoyed doing it.

Caleb remembered the red jets writhing under the water.

Screaming and jittering in place for a moment before frantically running to the tub, he'd slipped on the diluted pink blood she'd splashed onto the tiles, even as she gestured for him to come closer. She smiled at him, and that was still the worst thing he'd ever seen in his life. There were heaps of bubbles sloshing around, and the red was like syrup that had been spattered into the tub. He was barefoot and went skidding as he reached out and almost touched her hair.

Some of it was still so clear that Cal had to

open his eyes wide to keep himself from tripping back in time and place. He'd been impressed with the size of his sister's naked breasts, horrified and gagging in utter disbelief that the moment was real—and that this flow of venom had been stored inside her.

"Cal . . ."

His name on her lips sounded like a death scream or an ancient curse. It stopped him from going any closer.

Twin jets sprayed across the room as she lifted her hand from the water to grasp him. The blood shot forward and went coursing down the mirror to puddle in the toothbrush tray.

At the sight of it his palms opened up as though nails had been driven through his hands.

Spuming froth spattered his face and blinded him as he wheeled aside. He watched as both his sister's and his own streams of blood ran into one another. There was something lovely about it, really, as if they were rushing forward to help each other. The blood could do what he himself could not. No longer shrieking, almost curious now as his knees gave out and he finished going into shock, Caleb stared down at the gaping wounds in his hands and pitched face forward against the dripping shower faucet.

When he awoke in the hospital he had a concussion, and his sister had been in the ground for two days.

But that red stench had been planted way down deep inside his throat. He weakly tried to scrape out the back of his tongue with his fingernails. There were no wounds, scars, or marks on his hands, and nobody believed him when he explained what had happened.

That didn't bother him much anymore. Caleb had suffered through stigmata twice since then, his palms spontaneously imitating the wounds of the crucified Christ, ragged holes appearing in his hands. He wondered why the nail marks didn't go through his feet as well, or his side, where the Roman soldier had speared Christ on Golgotha, and why his scalp didn't drip from a thousand scratches of a bramble crown. If it was going to be done, it ought to be done right.

But it wasn't. He studied the phenomenon and learned it only occurred in the most devout, orthodox followers. So why him? And why then? There was madness to it, of course.

Caleb had been in his high school calculus class when his mother was killed in a car accident about a mile from home. His palms had burst open over a series of hyperbolic equations. It happened again when he was nineteen as he'd showered after an intermural racquetball tournament, on the day his father's bad heart finally gave out.

Cal knew they were dead long before anyone had a chance to tell him.

Massaging his knees, he'd stared at the peach-painted wall, and Fruggy Fred snored himself awake with one gigantic wheeze, glanced up, and said, "You'll find out, you'll put it together," then turned over and went back to sleep.

Caleb had known blood.

After hobbling to the campus security office, he found that it had been much easier to get them to tell him what had occurred in his room over Christmas vacation than he would've thought. He had expected the lies to start right off.

The two senior security officers were brothers, Wallace "Bull" Winkle and Michael "Rocky" Winkle, each man in his mid-forties, with silver-gray crew cuts mostly hidden beneath baseball caps, veins bulging in their temples, and their scowls usually soldered in place. They appeared so genuinely evil that even if you knew them to be upright guys, they still always made you think twice about it.

Rocky liked flipping troublemakers over his hip and throwing them headfirst into the nearest piece of furniture, like the dorm television set, and Bull just chopped them in their throats, wham, with the thickly callused side of his hand and then dragged them out into the street while they gagged. Cal had had a few run-ins with them over the years, usually when Fruggy Fred passed out in the middle of his show and Cal and Willy took over the radio station.

Fruggy would drop onto a cot and hit the alpha state in two meditative minutes flat. Willy would call up the hottest sounding girls they knew, no matter what they looked like, just so long as they hit a properly wicked timbre—and then put them on the air trying to get those luscious voices to tell stories along the lines of *Hustler* letters and Howard Stern. Inflections counted. To Rose's irritation, Willy had this thing about female body builders, and kept putting in long-distance calls to the editors of *Mother Muscle Magazine*, taunting ladies who could bench press 320 to come visit him, until Bull or Rocky showed up and tapped on the window and made a kill-it flick across the throat.

Caleb knew blood. So did Rocky and Bull, and you could tell it was something personal with them too. They sure as hell didn't like the idea that a teenager had been killed at the university, where it was their job to keep everyone safe. When Cal bounded in on his crutches he saw how their already beady eyes had fallen back even farther into their heads.

Bull waved a hand flatly across the air, scissoring conversation. He said, "Look, there's enough trouble on the first day of school. You, I don't need breaking my hump right now."

Caleb just looked at him. "Me?"

"I know what you want to say and I can understand everything you feel, but you're only going to make it worse."

"Me?"

"This office is working closely with the local police. We'll get to the bottom of it. That's all you need to know at the moment." An implied insult came through, as if to say that if Cal couldn't handle being in his room after a murder, he didn't have any guts. It pissed him off, but he squelched the anger. "What, you don't have any friends you ought to be out with tonight? What are you looking at?"

"What was her name?" Cal asked.

"Ah, goddamn it," Rock said. "Look, it gets unbearably boring over the intersession, hardly any people on campus at all, nothing happening anywhere, and you walk the buildings and dorms like always in the freezing weather, checking doors, making sure the kids who work the security desks check IDs and driver's licenses, and hoping they call ahead before letting a visitor in." Rocky seemed to take a surprised satisfaction in opening up, even though none of this had anything to do with her name. "They let their friends through without following the rules, and sometimes get sloppy and let others in, and don't call ahead."

"I know that," Cal said.

"You know shit," Bull said. "You think you've got it all down because you've been here for four years, but you don't understand much outside the classroom. What, you're going to argue? This is our home as much as it is yours, and we treat this campus like it's our place, too, and don't you forget it." Cal wouldn't forget it, or the fact that they were so shaken up about this that they were giving him mostly double-talk, wired and ready to go off at any second. "There've been rough times when jilted boyfriends come looking for trouble, and get passed through anyway, and somebody gets hurt. Date rape's up thirty-five percent. Death threats are too. The real thing I'm talking, when some loony kid goes after a teacher. Six physical assaults of that variety in the past couple of semesters. It gets worse every year."

"I know," Cal said.

Rocky continued. He was the one who appeared to have a tale to unburden, a weight slung on his back, so he must've been the one who found her. "So I wandered the halls and I saw that the door was ajar. I knocked and got no answer, walked in and saw her slumped in the corner. That's it. You'd think there was more to tell, some action to it, like me chasing after somebody, but there was nobody around. That's all there was. Just a dead girl."

"What was her name?" Cal whispered. He didn't even hear himself and had to say it again. He felt as if he were moving along a circle, seeing himself up ahead and way back behind, going nowhere.

"Sylvia Campbell," Rocky said.

"What'd they do to her?"

Bull gave a disgusted, I-dare-you grimace and managed to put it into his voice, too, running his words together and barely opening his mouth. "What are you gonna do?"

Rocky tried for the same kind of look and couldn't quite come up with it. "Get out of here, Prentiss."

"Not yet."

"Go."

"No, not yet. You couldn't have left me a note?"

"A note? Is that what you said? You wanted a note?"

"To have been informed."

Bull made a sudden movement, as if to startle a small animal, the calluses clearly seen as his chopping fist rose. "Go on!"

"What'd they do to her?"

Things could go on like this for a while, but maybe they knew something about him by now—everybody had to have a file here someplace—and he raised his crutches a little defensively. He wondered how far he'd get if they tried to remove him now, and whether he could swing the crutch hard enough and get a clean shot at one of the brothers, or if he'd already made his point.

"She was cut open," Rocky said, steadily glowering, more for Bull's sake than anyone's. "You still want that note? Details maybe? Slide it under your door or just use a stick-'em?"

Cal's sweaty palms kept slipping off the grips. "How long was she dead before you found her?"

"Coroner's report never came directly back to us, so as far as the state is concerned we're merely citizens with no official peace officer capacity. But my guess is twenty-four hours."

"Jesus, God," Cal said, thinking of her being alone that long *with the fucking door unlocked*. There were 200 other people in the dorm. "Where are the reporters, the Channel Three film crews?" he asked. Mary Grissom's caps flashed him, and he saw Buffy holding Mrs.

Beasley under her arm. "What about the other kids? Why the hell didn't anyone say anything about it?"

Rocky glared. "Say? What the hell were they going to say?"

Bull jerked his shoulders into a shrewd shrug. "Same old story, what else? People lead busy lives, there's not a lot of time to be especially curious about a stranger. The other kids in the dorm probably just thought somebody's tuna casserole had been left out a little too long."

The comment took Caleb low in the belly and made him wobble and grunt. "You rotten son of a bitch!"

"Hey, fuck you, Prentiss. What, did you know her? Where were you celebrating Christmas, huh? You had nowhere to go, right? I know you didn't. So what, did you hide out around here? You come back a little early? Find a girl in your bed that wouldn't play ball?"

"That's cute."

Veins in Bull's temples pulsed as though insects crawled under his skin. "What do you think this is, a cover-up like in a movie? Everybody in on it except you? You want a note. Who the fuck are you? Didn't you read the papers? It's there. Where were you, Prentiss?"

"No, I didn't see the papers."

"Or the television reports?"

"No."

"Then how the hell did you know it was a girl, huh? You kept asking what *her* name was."

"I just assumed."

"My ass you did!" Bull shouted. "Where were you?"

Rocky cut in, maybe to disarm the moment or maybe because he didn't know how close to the edge they were getting. Caleb felt that they were right up there, to the line. "We've been interviewed by Channel Three and every place else for weeks. Got my kisser on page fourteen myself. It's just starting to die down. We've got increased security. You haven't seen more police patrolling? You gonna stir it back up?"

"Why haven't the cops questioned me? It was my room."

Bull kept peering at him. "You think you own it? A hundred students have lived in that room. You just go to school here, kid."

Yes, it was true, this was only school.

"It's the first day back," Rocky offered. "The police will be on you, don't worry about that. They'll question you until your eyes roll. As for the rest . . . well, nobody's going to come back here after baking Christmas cookies and going down to Florida for vacation and immediately talk about some gutted girl."

Yes, they would. Of course they would. If they knew.

"It's no secret. Where've you been?"

That really was the question, as if he had put the final, fatal spin on this turn of events himself. He'd made a mistake. He should have been here. It was his room. He said, "The gossip still would've been everywhere on campus by now, or at least all over the dorm. Everybody would be stopping by my place just to take a glimpse inside. My friends didn't even know about it."

"You sure?" Bull asked. "You think you know about every night stalker rape that happens in this town? On this campus?"

"Look, I just want . . ."

"How many funerals did you go to last year? How many condolence cards did you send? Did you know every hit-and-run victim? Did you know the kids who died of cancer and leukemia? Do you really care?"

He couldn't find the spit to swallow. "Yes, I do."

"No, you don't. You never have. You didn't even know Sylvia Campbell, and you only give a damn now because you got the heebie-jeebies, because it happened right under your own nose."

"Yours too."

"Fuck you, kid."

"I know how the dean works. He hushed this thing up. He had to."

"And what else would you expect? You want him to plaster the fact everywhere, show it off to all the parents at orientation? You'd get a real kick out of that, now wouldn't you. Put a neon arrow aimed at your room, charge five bucks to have folks come look at the bed."

The grips of his crutches were beginning to crack. He tried to ease up and unclench his fists, but he couldn't really swing it.

"The police believe the perp had it in for the girl and the girl alone," Rocky said. " 'An isolated incident' is the term they throw. If it wasn't a random killing, they figure it was probably an argument that got out of hand between her and her boyfriend, or some weird one-night stand that went too far, some guy she picked up in town, which is what I personally believe it was. This place was so lonely, you have no idea what people will do."

With his legs buckling, Cal knew he had to get out of the office fast before someone got flipped into the furniture. "And if it wasn't, Rocky?" he asked under his breath, turning to leave. "Thanks for being straight with me; I appreciate it." That was the truth, though they both looked at him as if he were lying. "One more thing: What if this guy's still around?"

He wondered if there'd been other murders on campus during other intercessions he didn't know about.

"What, you worried he'll come back and knock you off?" Bull asked. "You think maybe somebody had it in for you and thought she was your girlfriend and just missed his chance at you so he went for her instead?"

He hadn't thought of that. He hadn't thought of that at all. "No."

"Well, maybe you should."

"Shut up," he told himself again, running the heels of his hands against his eyes as he shifted sideways in Sylvia Campbell's love seat.

Like claws, the branches just outside scratched at the storage room window again, snapping his attention back to his surroundings. He took the index card out of his wallet and stared at Sylvia Campbell's lovely face as the freezing rain began to slash down against the glass.

Me.

Chapter Five

Why did you lie?

Caleb glanced at his notes without reading them, waiting for the threads of answers to appear.

The silence, which had irked him just a few minutes ago, now had a soothing effect, lulling him while the windows rattled. Wind groaned like an appeased lover. Macbeth came to mind. *Come you spirits, that tend on mortal thoughts, unsex me here.* He didn't much like the *unsex me* part, but the rest of it sounded right.

A week ago he'd fallen asleep here in the storage room and awoken with the jagged feeling that he'd dreamed a long continuous cycle of dreams he couldn't remember. It nagged at him but was better than the nightmares.

He carefully put the sketch back in his pocket, ignoring the dust, finding solace in the chill. It could work for you on occasion, if you let it. He sniffed, seeking trace chemicals of her lingering fragrance, trying to discover her skin, hair, and flavor. There had been flecks of fingernail polish, three strands of brown hair, and a faint scent of flowers in the mattress. Chrysanthemums or violets. Fading perfume or fancy soap, incense or air freshener? He couldn't be sure. Beneath it all remained what had been found in his own bed.

Duncan is in his grave; After life's fitful fever he sleeps well. Pages of his notes wafted to the floor. They were more a part of her than of him. Rolling on his back, he looked at the printouts of her transcripts, which he'd tucked between chapters of his thesis.

For the past couple of semesters Rose had worked in the registrar's office. On occasion, after Willy and Caleb had been thrown out of the KLAP station and the women weightlifters were disconnected, they'd visit with her at the bursar's office. Scanning their own records, incapable of breaking into the encoded stuff but getting a kick out of trying anyway, Rose would read off some of the more scathing comments from their professors. Willy always laughed it off, but Caleb would stare at the files and see his worst grades glaring back.

"Howard Moored, my ENG 101 professor, says I have a ninth-grade reading comprehension," Willy said.

"He's being kind."

"What's *Catcher in Your Eye?*"

"Uhm, good question."

"Come on, that's tenth grade, isn't it? Hey, I read that. Howard shortchanged me."

Rose would look at Willy with the deepest respect and love anyway, knowing she'd never sign him up for any book clubs.

Violets or chrysanthemums.

After talking with Rocky and Bull that first day, Caleb eyed the peach paint for hours while making pitiful conversation with Willy and Rose, wondering if he could stay in his own place anymore—if it was his place or ever had been—and if he had that kind of endurance. When they'd finally gone, it took until nearly midnight before he could touch the stained spot on the wall, reaching out tentatively to move his fingers along the indistinct outline beneath the paint. You could draw pictures for hours with it, like looking at clouds.

There were knives in the air. Still on the bed, Fruggy Fred mumbled in his dream-wracked sleep. He stirred with infrequent urgency, muttering and groping, imploring, as if giving Caleb cryptic warnings. Sometimes he sobbed until his beard was drenched and heavy with salt. Every so often his hands would flash out and he'd call Cal's name. The new mattress looked too white beneath Fruggy. Cal pondered what they'd done with the old one.

The phone rang. It was Jodi, and before he could make up his mind what to tell her, about the stink in his room and the world abruptly taking on a new shape, she'd inhaled so deeply he knew she was about to yell at him. It was nice to be able to get ready for it. He immediately apologized and promised to drop by later on, and let the rest of it go.

"Later?" she asked. "It's already almost midnight. I've been looking for you all day. Where have you been?"

"Here."

"No, you weren't. I stopped by and your door was locked. I've called a half dozen times the past couple of hours."

"Jesus, don't say that." He hadn't heard it. Maybe Fruggy had just been telling him to answer the phone.

"It's our first night together after so long, when my parents finally aren't lurking about, watching us like ospreys, and without the babies around. What's the matter? You sound strange."

"Do I? I'm sorry." See? . . . She didn't know about any murders. "What have you been doing today?"

"I'm the one who's sorry, but I'm always apologizing for the way they treat you. And me."

One more time around that track. She could no more let go of her family than he could his. "They didn't have to take me in, but they did, for a while. That counts for something." He'd learned to be appreciative to those who showed him any kindness, even if he had to look after the deformed offspring of prostitutes and reefer hustlers to earn such treatment.

"It should, but it usually doesn't when it counts. Not when it keeps us apart like that, in that ugly kind of way. It's been a hell of a new year so far. I received notice that two of my classes didn't go through; there's been some kind of screwup."

"Not PHILO 138?" he asked. It had been their one shared class on the same side of the quad, and he'd heard Professor Yokver was excellent. Ethics should be a breeze, and he figured to go out with an easy semester before getting torn up outside in the big world.

"No, we'll still have our mornings together in that one." Her husky voice, weighty with sex, purred in his ear, but he could hear the underlying anger from his lack of enthusiasm. They hadn't been in bed together for over a month. She wanted to know why the hell he hadn't been crouched outside her door, crazy from lust, the minute they got back to campus. He wasn't doing much to make her feel needed. She said, "I'll be over in five minutes."

He held his head out the window, the meat locker stink abruptly upon him as Fruggy mumbled again, mentioning Jodi's name in a sigh, then making some of the same noises he'd made while climbing outside the dorm naked. "Uh, I'd rather come to your place, Jo."

Cal could almost see the frown. "Why?" she asked, a pregnant hesitation as she ran through any number of possible problems.

There was a long checklist. He could tell she was going through them, one by one, remembering how he'd staggered onto her porch with his crutches, hands slashed. How twelve hours ago her father drove her back to the university in his pickup without a word of departure to Cal, leaving him there on the lawn packing up his gear, flea-gnawed dogs barking everywhere and the babies wailing. It was simply the man's policy to let Caleb know just where they all stood, without any need to explain, as the hydrocephalic children came outside and teetered on the porch.

Johnny had finished painting the Toyotas lemon yellow, and they glared in the sunlight on proud display. Russell had packed the backseats full of women's shoes and clock radios, sitting there on the hood of one while flipping through a *Reader's Digest*, reading the jokes aloud to himself.

Allowing Caleb to live in the yard hadn't been an invitation; it was a presentation of power. Jo's mother had come onto him a couple of times, and maybe this was the father's style of showing Cal that he couldn't have everything all the time. Jodi had gotten into the passenger seat while her father revved the engine and made a mud doughnut wheeling out of the yard. The retarded babies all ran for it.

"Is anything wrong, Cal?" she asked, and her voice suddenly seemed tinny, buzzing in his ear.

"No, Jodi." His own voice was firm and stable, underscored by Fruggy's wheezing. Odd that he didn't sound like he was going crazy. "Nothing's wrong."

"You sure?"

Orphaned once more, he'd started to hobble the two miles to the bus station, with the hydrocephalic kids leaning their swollen heads against the peeling paint of the porch rails and grinning at him, Johnny high and nodding on the stoop, Russell still trying to make it through the first page of jokes and not getting very far, everybody brittle and perishing.

He said, "It's just that Fruggy Fred is asleep over here, and I don't think he's going to be able to make it back to his own room tonight."

"Well, kick his fat ass out of there!"

"I think . . . he's sick, and I just want to make sure he's all right."

"Walk him over to the infirmary. It's right on the way."

"You know better than that, Jo. It would be like interrupting Midnight Mass. This is a sacred ritual."

"I don't give a damn about his beauty sleep. Since when are you the watchdog for that zombie?"

"C'mon, don't talk about him that way." She didn't understand that when Fruggy slept, he *moved* and went places.

"He's a complete waste product whom you've been valiantly trying to put on a pedestal, like he was a mystic of some sort, Buddha beneath his Bo tree, as if he might actually be meditating . . ."

"Listen—"

". . . instead of being in a . . . a tumult of psy-

chotic depression that leaves him nearly co-
matose. When you weight nearly four hundred
pounds and close yourself off socially to the few
friends you have, that's what happens. He ought
to be on medication and a strict diet, not being
coddled by you." She tried to let it go, and let
out a long breath through her nostrils that went
on a lot longer than he expected it to. "Forget
it, just come on over, please. Please, let's not
fight."

When he got there and set eyes on her, after
already having had his head stuffed with new
blood and old, his love and longing welled inside him, anchored somehow by humiliation.
He remembered his sorrow, and his sorrow remembered him. Jodi shut off her lamps and
held him, slow dancing as the glowing moon
started its dive over their shoulders. He tossed
his crutches in the corner and let himself lean
against her, as she held him up.

"I thought you might be mad at me," she
whispered. "For something." She bit her lower
lip and struck what she thought was her little
girl pouting pose, nothing the least bit similar
to a child in her face. It started doing things to
him.

"Never."

"Not even for the awful time you had at my
house?"

"It wasn't that bad."

"Thanks for not turning in my brothers."

"They'll get theirs eventually. It just has to happen that way."

She let that slide too, because she could never take her family head on, they scared the shit out of her. "Then for something else?"

"No."

"I don't think I can believe that."

"You doubt my veracity?" Cal asked.

"Well," she said, "you've certainly got your own agenda, pal." Sometimes when she used the *pal* it came off like a cop moving a homeless man out of a train station, the old *Move it along, pal*, but not now. "And you haven't seen fit to let me in. The insurance money you got from your parents won't last forever, although you don't want to acknowledge that fact."

She was right about that. "Uhm."

"You have to fill out résumés, get a job, an apartment. Do you have any notion what you'll do after graduation? Where or how you'll live?"

"Ah."

He wondered if she was about to add that he couldn't come back home with her ever again; he'd sort of miss the retarded kids. Suddenly she heaved, fighting back a massive sob. "You have to give in on occasion."

"Give in?"

"You can't keep fighting everyone, always coloring outside the lines."

"I think we're mixing our metaphors." He chuckled to shield himself from her intuition, or maybe to protect her. Did he color outside the lines? Had he ever? He could feel her comprehension as if he were a patient having his X-rays examined, all his Rorschachs being held up and studied for significance.

You see a black-necked Grebe perched on the left shoulder of Trotsky? . . . tsk tsk.

She nuzzled him then, running her fingers through his hair with slow, careless caresses. "You're so distant tonight."

"Sorry."

"You don't have to apologize." He almost did it again. "Yes, I know, we're both sorry, but I want you to talk to me."

"I tell you whatever I can tell you, Jo," he lamented. She drifted across the room to her desk.

"That is not, as they say, an adequate answer, Cal," she told him.

"It is, as I say, all I've got."

That wasn't nearly enough, but at least it was out on the plate. Darkness promised to contain their secrets. She had them too, something to do with why a preschooler should have perfect handwriting, living in that house of recessive genes. He sensed that she shuffled hidden feelings beneath other more open emotions. That troubled him, but there was nothing to do.

She sat in the chair with her feet kicked up on the windowsill, tapping out a nice salsa rhythm. They heard parties going on along the floor, KLAP playing Zenith Brite music turned full volume, shrieks and laughter in the halls. There were loud splashes of beer, and girls crying. It would go on like this for days.

Jodi kept bringing up her fear of slipping grades, too worried even before classes had started, telling him the push for med school was wearing her down. He knew school actually excited her, and that it was he who proved to be her real burden. Soles of her bare feet slapped the windowpane glass. Every time he saw a revelation surge inside Jodi, about to come forward, he would silently plead for her to say it, just say it, but she never took that step, and it always came back to grades.

She sat with him on the bed. Her hand flopped against his leg and lazily drew lines down his inner thigh. He'd once had to dissect a piglet for a sophomore biology lab, and knew that next year in med school she'd be doing the same to corpses. Strange, the connections you can make. Moonlight glanced off Jodi's forehead.

"Cal, this isn't a party anymore," she said. People cheered next door, and the weeping became louder. She spoke in his ear as matter-of-factly as possible, the way she did to the hydrocephalic kids. "I've already told you all the stories . . ." Yes, she had, and he'd seen it for himself up close, of how her father had scarred her mom, that nose with an extra curve in it now, and how they'd all found solace in the bottle, brothers stealing beer for the mother, children kneeling around hoping she would pass out. As bad as it was, he still wondered if it was worse than being an orphan. She said, "I can't backslide into that after these past years of such a haul."

"Do you think that's what I want?"

"No, but I'm only away from the trailer trash because of my scholarships, and if I slip, I can only skid back to them, and I'm so close to getting out."

"You are out."

"No, not yet."

He didn't have the words. "Jodi—"

She trembled as he held her. "I won't live and die like that," she told him sadly, as if already knowing just how she'd live and die. He thought of telling her of the blood in his room then, but couldn't go through with it.

Touching his cheek gently, she buried her

face in his chest and shook without crying. It was the same motion she made when she had an orgasm, and he started to get horny. Jo raised her head and started to say something more, but he was tired of all this and sealed his mouth over hers.

Soon they were naked, distress emphasized by need. In the little more than a year that they'd been lovers he'd never felt less secure than he did at that moment. The thought of losing her drove him nearly out of his mind, as did the sound of his sister saying prayers in the darkness.

Long blond hair cascaded over his chest as she mounted him, and the presence of death moved aside for an instant, forced out beneath Jodi's hands. She whimpered and bent forward over him, making a tent of her hair so that they were face-to-face and hidden under here, biting his neck and drawing blood that smeared the corner of her bottom lip. He left pink tracks over her skin from his scabbed hands. His knees were killing him. Jodi groaned, their rhythm moving faster than he wanted, and she gasped and yelped into his chest as they erupted together too soon.

Their movements slowed without ever actually having truly started, occasionally shuddering but continuing on into the afterplay, until

Jo rolled off. She spun to face him with her eyes closed tightly, fingers working weakly over his sweaty arms. She kissed him fiercely and he crushed her to him. Her hair was everywhere—in his eyes, against his lips, tickling his nostrils. Sweat pooled in her navel. An hour ago she'd smelled of perfume, and now she reeked of nothing other than Caleb Prentiss.

Chrysanthemums.

The storage room grew colder and rain snapped at the window. He reached and gathered his notes from where they lay spread on the floor, rereading the data, sifting through his story line again. He lifted his thesis and felt its significant weight, understanding the irony of just how thinly sliced a life could get. He must've had something to say, but he didn't know what.

Knots of the wicker seat tortured his back as he stared at the file sheets. They stated Sylvia Campbell's name and gave a regional address and number, average grades from the local high school. Transcripts verified that the intersession course had consisted of her first three college credits. It made sense—if she had to miss the fall semester, for whatever reason, she might have wanted to catch up on lost time by attending the accelerated intersession before the spring semester began.

But why only the one class? Intersession courses were difficult, but if you were going to be on campus studying your ass off over winter break anyway, you'd be better off with two or even three classes. It could be done, but you'd need the dean's permission first.

After leaving Jodi that next morning Cal felt a sharpness of purpose he hadn't felt during the night. Classes started slow, the workload light, and he remained on friendly terms with most of his professors. There was no buzz about psychos stalking kids, and no film students planning on doing a horror feature on his room. Nobody came by to see where Sylvia Campbell had died, and in a way that saddened him a little.

He went to the library and checked rolls of microfiche, reading the past weeks' newspapers to find out what he could about Sylvia Campbell. They reported the incident in relatively graphic detail, though her name hadn't been released in print until relatives could be contacted. It was puzzling that Rocky would have told him. Later issues covered little else. Hadn't they found her family yet, or didn't she have one?

Willy questioned him as they lifted weights in the gym, Cal's hands raw but his legs feeling better after having gotten laid. Except for his knees he was in the best shape of his life.

"What the hell was that all about in your room last night? You kind of freaked me out there for a while." Willy's chest and stomach muscles rippled like tectonic plates shifting. "Something happened in the Combat Zone, right? I mean, you can't be bored already. You and Jodi didn't even show for Rose's little get-together last night. Is there some trouble on that front?"

Nobody had noticed the stain on the wall and no one had picked up on the stench—that was the place to start with the thesis. Comment on how easily ignored your own murder can be. How nobody watches carefully enough, except maybe for Fruggy Fred. "You could say that."

"Eh," Willy said.

"That's what I like best about you. It's got to be your unerring ability to give good advice."

"You want advice?"

"Hell no."

"That's what I figured." A quake in Willy's torso as his pecs and lats rippled. "I'll spare you a rehash of platitudes, because if you aren't happy, then you came to the right man for answers."

"How's a guy with a ninth-grade reading comprehension know a word like *platitudes?*" How does he even stay in school?

"I told you, I got gypped. Now, do you want me to tell you how the key to happiness can be yours? I can do it, you know."

No no, not again. Willy had this idea that he was actually a sex therapist with a wall of Ph.D.s and kept trying to get his own show on KLAP. "Is that so?"

Weird, but Willy actually looked and sounded serious. "So it is indeed. Listen to the doctor when he talks. Forget whatever happened to you over vacation, and all the stress being brought on by our impending graduation. It is time for you get hopelessly crazed and take advantage of our first couple days back, when everybody's still juiced."

"Is that what they are?"

"You wouldn't know. You never notice. Take this special lady I'll be seeing tonight—"

Gasping for air, Caleb staggered in doing his curls, the weight bar hitting him hard in the chest as he brought it up. He gave a grunt as if punched, biceps burning and rivulets of sweat parting his hair. "Jesus, God," he whispered. His squint narrowed to slits he could barely see through. Somebody was missing the point. *I haven't noticed.* Was he just as guilty?

Willy barked a vain and arrogant laugh, thinking that Cal was proud or in awe of him, sleeping with the lovely Rose and now some special lady as well. Willy should know better than to screw around.

"If Rose catches you, all the iron thews in the world won't save you from a real ass whipping."

"Rose is not exactly all my woman."

"That's a load of shit," Cal said.

"We have an open relationship."

"Listen, that's the dumbest thing I've ever heard you say, not counting the *Catcher in your Eye* comment."

"Hey, you may have known her longer, but I know her better. I love her, man, but we've never let it get too serious. Great sex and fun, good friends . . . best friends, in fact. I really do love her, that's no lie. But so far as anything else . . . we pretty much don't talk about it."

It felt as though he were actually the one being cheated on. "If you don't talk, then you don't understand her."

"Listen . . . don't start telling me—"

"I'm not starting anything."

"Yes, you are. You're judgmental, you always have been." Willy shook his head and smiled, arms curling perfectly, mechanically, straining yet removed from the man talking, and showing no pain. "This other thing is new, and the situation is exciting. And that's what it's all about."

"If you say so. Who is she?"

Shucking the curling bar, Willy began military presses with enough weight to snap most guys' spines. Sweat flew against the mats in a dull pitter-patter. "I've got to plead the Fifth on that."

"Why?"

"Believe me, you'd never understand."

Willy never pleaded the Fifth on anything, but Cal did believe him. "If it's Jodi, I'll kill you," he said. "Not bare-handed, to be sure, but maybe with a few well-placed land mines."

Face innocent, mushy furrowed brows like a basset hound, Willy implored, "Would I do that to you? Nah, don't answer that, you paranoid nut. She wouldn't do it to you either, sleeping with your friend. The woman in question is not your damsel, be she in distress or not, and I still ain't going to say."

Good; Cal really didn't want to know anyway. "How are you able to talk so much when you lift?"

"You go into it and then you go through it." Still no pain; this was Willy's way of having fun. He repeatedly raised the bar slowly over his head, his face red but his eyes extremely clear. "Proper breathing and positive mental attitude."

"Oh."

"Plenty of vegetables and fish. Strong old-fashioned family values in tandem with a firm

Christian upbringing. Powerful spiritual beliefs in the love and mercy of our lord Hey-seuss Kee-rist." He took deep, efficient breaths. Across his entire upper body protruded veins that drew a topographical map of routes to Florida. "Now, as I said before, this lady I speak of is special. So exceptional, in fact, that if anyone found out about our love nest it would mean *beaucoup de* bad news. *Capisce, amigo?*"

"Ever the linguist. You sound like you're in love with her."

"No," Willy said, followed by nothing. He finished his rep of twenty, corded muscles of his back and shoulders as defined as any ancient Grecian statue. "If you want to nail Rose, you know, that's okay with me."

Cal stared at him.

"It is," Willy said.

"What?"

"You already know I'm not the jealous type. Have a blast. Just be good to her. Don't get too nutty. I know that's difficult for you, but try your best."

Okay, now what the hell was this? A peace offering or just another way to bond? "That's not it."

"Something's it."

"Correct," Cal said.

"And you won't talk?"

"Everybody's got a little to hold back nowa-days, it seems."

Willy sighed in agreement. "The rest of the world impedes."

Impedes was another good word for a guy with only a ninth-grade reading comprehen-sion. Howard apparently really had ripped Willy off a grade or two. "Yes, I suppose it does." It could impede upon you in the middle of the night, in your own bed. It could impale you.

"It's our sin for seeking to eventually leave these hollowed halls. The university gets jeal-ous."

"Hallowed."

"What?"

"Nothing."

"Anyway, we've got a few months left and I intend to use them to the fullest. You?"

"Me," Caleb said.

They'd showered, left the gym, and gone over to see Rose at the registrar's office. As she and Willy laughed and made out against the desk, Cal had gotten onto the computer and gone through the student files, searching for a copy of Sylvia Campbell's application records and transcripts. You didn't have to be a hacker to call them up. He typed her name out with a soft touch, referencing all university material, and watched as the screen flashed PLEASE WAIT at him . . . telling him to ease up there, boy, you're a little too full of yourself lately . . . PLEASE WAIT. . . . Settle down, this isn't any of your god-damn business, after all, and you even got a new mattress out of the deal, so just who the fuck do you think you are, anyway? . . . PLEASE WAIT . . . if you want it, this is the proof that you, too, will be bled dry if you're in the right place at the wrong time, and yeah, you might even be next, just keep sleeping there with your head against the pillow, the pillow on the bed, the bed against the wall, the wall that's been painted . . . PLEASE WAIT, YOU LITTLE SHIT . . . are you sure you really want to go through with this?

Until at last Sylvia Campbell's records kicked onto the screen.

He keyed the printer and grabbed the sheets without looking, folded and stuck them in his pocket as Rose and Willy continued kissing, not noticing anything he'd been doing, and he watched them, wondering how it would all play out. Whatever happened, there was going to be a hell of a lot of trouble. He could imagine Willy on the floor clutching his stomach, winding his viscera around his fingers, Rose disheveled and standing over him with a cleaver in her hand, shrieking, "So, you thought this was an open relationship, you asshole?"

When he got back to his dorm Caleb peeled the papers apart like a starving monkey opening a banana. According to the sheets, Sylvia Campbell had graduated from the local high school, about middle of her class. She'd lived in town her entire life—so then why skip the fall semester? No cash, had to work? She'd come into the intersession to take three credits of an independent project.

With Professor Yokver.

Caleb had believed you could only take credit projects after your sophomore year. He sought out her home address, checking the map and finding it was thirty minutes away through town on foot. He walked it with an even pace, without the crutches. What could he possibly say to Sylvia's parents? *Mrs. Campbell, you don't know me, but . . . what's that, ma'am? . . . No, I'm not the Fuller Brush salesman; no, no, not a cop or a reporter either; no, not her friend. I'd just like to talk to you about your daughter, you know the one. The dead one. See, we shared the same bed. No, ma'am, nothing like that, see, it's just that . . .* He thought a lot about madness and genetics as he walked across the sleet-filled streets to her house.

Had the cops even been in touch with her parents yet? Sylvia's name still hadn't been released in the paper, so far as he could find. Was he going to stand on the doorstep and find her mother just back from some trip, down visiting her Aunt Philimina in Waykosha, Georgia, standing there in the living room with two pieces of luggage at her knees, phone in her hand to call Sylvia and ask how classes were going? Could he really look into that woman's face?

When he got there he found a service area/truck rest stop, half a mile from the main highway out of town. If he'd looked at the map more closely, he would have realized it. But he hadn't noticed.

Returning to the university in a dazed fog, the chill wind battered his knees. He entered his room and the blood stink welcomed him. Her home number had a reedy-voice recording: *"The number you have reached is not in service."*

Chrysanthemums.

Sylvia Campbell, age eighteen according to these lies in his hand, remained alive now in his memory. The cops would follow the trail and discover that she faked her transcripts and the university didn't bother to check. That should've been good enough for a little investigative journalism, but the papers never mentioned it.

He went back to the library and did some more checking, and found another three related

articles he'd skipped the first time because they
were in the "Jack-In" computer pull-out section
of the paper. They related how the faking of
transcripts was getting to be fairly common
across the nation, especially in poorer high
school districts where the computer systems
could easily be tampered with. The articles ba-
sically blamed Sylvia for giving the police so little to go on by falsifying her records. The
implication was that she'd initiated her murder
by her own criminal act.

Goddamn pricks.

Caleb questioned the resident administrator
until he got the name of the custodian who had
cleaned and painted the room. He discovered
where student property was kept. He set off a
fire alarm going into the sub-basement of the
library the first time, and wandered into other
storage rooms in the recesses of the tunnels,
checking room numbers until he came to where
the custodian said he'd left her personal belongings.

Grappling that night with the fence, he kicked
at the window frame from the outside until the
runners bent and the latch snapped. Someone
had dumped off her life and death like all the
crap shoved into your junk drawer. He wondered why the cops hadn't taken the rest of her
things in as evidence.

Without fully understanding why this mattered so much to him, he'd started writing his senior thesis:

The Death of Circe

He got the title from her signature, the tiny *Sy. C.* that put it into some perspective, as though he had to listen to this siren call of the sorceress, on his own odyssey. All of art is metaphor, Frost had said, and you couldn't get away from it. He'd never found any of her notebooks—no letters or diaries, poems, papers, test scores. No writing at all, nothing from her mind except the sketch. If the cops had it all, they hadn't done anything with it.

He would have to find out who killed her.

The gray outside reflected his own state of mind. Fair is foul and foul is fair. The cycle of his dreams had begun and ended once again. Caleb wasn't aware that he'd slept for three hours in the storage room lying in the love seat.

What do angels dream? He was certain she would answer him if he asked her enough times.

So he asked again.

And again.

And again.

Caleb left his coffin.

Chapter Six

By the time he got outside the rain had turned to snow.

Cal hopped the fence and marched up the embankment, facing into the wind heading back toward Camden Hall, the humanities building where he had most of his classes. The snow came down hard enough so that in a few minutes his footprints wouldn't be seen leading out from the window.

Passing in front of Camden Hall, Caleb literally ran into the dean and his wife.

Caught in his own thoughts, wiping his face, Cal didn't see the two figures coming toward him until it was too late. He turned and tried to evade—completing a tricky pirouette—but his legs gave out as he cut left. His kneecap cracked as the dean barreled into him, catching him painfully under the clavicle and driving in like a linebacker. A piercing twinge shot up Cal's shoulder as if he'd been struck with a scimitar.

In his maneuvering he slid against Lady Dean's mink coat; the softness of it was so warm and welcoming that he went with it for a second. The hell was she doing wearing mink in this kind of weather? His face brushed the fur as he tilted further, and he let out an odd sigh of relief, sort of going, "Hmmm." Her coat flew open as she took a step backward, and the palm of his hand landed with a solid thwack against her breasts.

The chill factor dropped another ten degrees. Their icily eminent gazes tagged him hard as he looked over to see them watching him closely.

The dean was the most inhuman-appearing man on campus, but somehow he still managed to be handsome, or nearly so, in an eerie way, some women had said. It was fascinating to watch the dean move his gaunt frame, the falling snow sort of bending, *weaving* around him. Always elegantly poised, he stood—what, maybe 6'8" or 9"? . . . Really up there, so that you had to tip your head back until it hurt, and his waving high-cropped black hair took him to about an inch over seven feet.

At fifty, the dean was a living cliché of the walking skeleton, emaciated to the point of being an Auschwitz survivor, with long sleek fingers that curved like meat hooks. Whenever Cal shook hands with him he got the heebie-jeebies. When the dean smoked a cigarette you couldn't keep your eyes off him, enthralled as he brought those hands further and further upwards to his lips, still going, still going, until he finally took a drag, and the stream of smoke dissipated long before it got to you. He would have made a good Rubber Man in a freak show, tying himself in knots of cartilage. He seemed to be ossifying where he stood, a pillar of ashen bone, as though two skeletons had been wedged together beneath a paper-thin coating of skin.

Cal grinned wanly. It hurt his neck, looking up and trying to meet the dean's eyes. "Hello."

Lady Dean's real name was Clarissa, but he could hardly ever remember. Whenever she glanced at him she made a face he couldn't completely describe. In four years he'd never seen her laugh, or even smile, with any kind of real emotion. Once or twice, in conversation, Cal had heard the birth scream of a giggle coming from her, and he'd waited to see it fully enter the world, only to hear the laugh die in utero as it was abruptly swallowed.

Strange to think she could appear so homely

when she was actually extremely attractive, the complete opposite of her husband's lovely ugliness. Younger than the dean—Cal judged her to be in her mid-thirties—she had a mean enough glare to make you wonder if she really felt such disdain or if she was only playing the temptress, cozying up to the masochist in everyone. His gut reaction was that she somehow wanted him to help her.

"Hello, Cal. It's been quite a while," she said. "Nice to see you again. I'm only sorry our meeting had to be coincidence." She took him by the hand and led him out of the falling snow, until they were under the stone arch of Camden's main entrance. The dean followed silently but with a lot to say etched into that gaunt face.

"Yes," Cal said, because there wasn't much else to say.

Lady Dean went on. "As this is your last semester, and you won't be with us much longer, let me say how much we've enjoyed your company, truly." She caught herself. He tried to find some sincerity in her face and came up pretty empty. "Really, I don't mean to make it sound as though your life's coming to an end. You've a whole extraordinary, challenging world awaiting, after you leave us."

"Perhaps I'll go for my masters," Cal said. "And my doctorate." Actually, nothing scared him more, except perhaps the whole extraordinary, challenging world out there waiting for him.

"Well, there's always room for another Doctor of English," she said, really going for the nerve. Sarcasm was not one of her better nuances. "Will you be stopping by our home this evening?"

"Your home?"

"Yes, we're having an informal get-together later on tonight. Nothing too extravagant."

"I see."

The dean cocked an eyebrow at his wife and showed a moment of surprise that vanished immediately. Cal knew the dean had meant for him to read it as such, each gesture of calculated purpose hidden and out in the open simultaneously, so that you could never be sure whether face value had any value at all. The dean's thread-fine lips twisted into a charming smile. It could raise your hackles.

Lady Dean tried to grin and failed so miserably that he felt bad for her. "I'd also like to speak privately with you, Cal. Do drop in on us later, won't you?"

It wasn't exactly a question. "I'll certainly try."

"And please bring along your lovely girlfriend as well." The Lady's fingers floated through the air, searching for Jodi's name, pinching and clenching here and there. Despite the fact that Jo remained introverted and generally despised the social circle of academia, she still played the game damn well. She'd made the dean's list four years straight and won nearly every award available. It was impossible the Lady didn't know her name. "Jenny?"

"Jodi."

"Yes, that's right, I recall now, how silly of me." The hand clutched again, straying toward Cal's chin. "Jodi. Shall we say . . . at around seven? Or seven-thirty." The content of her voice hacked through any rebuff.

"Without fail."

"Wonderful."

Caleb nodded and watched them walk off, their regal manner giving them a sort of slow-motion fade-out as they drifted into the swirling snow.

He went to Jo's dorm. The kid on duty at the security desk didn't even look up from his calculus textbook, solid metal door slamming shut loudly as Cal walked in. The equations on the page reminded him of those he'd been doing at the time of his mother's death. Geometrically comparing the mapping properties of a function with those of its linear approximation. Non-differentiable surfaces, and arguing why the cube root of (x^3-3xy^2) fails to be differentiable at the origin. He wondered how his life would have turned out if he'd been only one integer off at birth.

The conversation he'd had with Bull and Rocky three weeks earlier came back to him in full. About how the kids working the security desks were too lazy, and killers could waltz in at any time and you wouldn't know it until you got into the shower. You're just standing here and he hasn't even looked up yet. You could have an Uzi, a dripping cleaver, twelve sticks of dynamite taped to your chest, and still get no reaction. Cal scowled at the top of the guy's buzz cut and thought about making a scene. The image came too close to that of the railing Yok to sit well.

Slapping his college ID card on top of the calculus text, Cal said in his best Lady Dean voice, "You're supposed to make sure these premises are secure from any unwanted or unknown persons. You start by making eye contact and checking student identification."

The guy glanced up, but that was about it. His eyes were filled with vectors and matrices. "What? What do you want?"

"Come on, man, don't make it so easy for them."

"Easy for them? For who?"

"For *them*. For *him*."

109

"What the hell are you talking about?"

"Stay alert and do your job."

"What job? Listen, you got a problem? I don't have to take crap from you. What room number are you going to? Hey . . ."

Cal headed to the stairway, slipped up the three flights to her room, and rapped his distinctive knock on the door, a sort of jazzy rappit-tappity riff with both sets of knuckles.

Jodi answered with a worried frown, her hair messed into a crazed bouffant. Her blouse was partially untucked, one sleeve rolled to her elbow and the other loose at the wrist. In twenty-five years this would be a haggard pose, the drunken horror that was her mother, but right now she looked sensually disarrayed. Yanking a handful of hair out of her eyes and mouth, she said, "Who in the hell have you been on the phone with all day? Or did you leave it off the hook?"

He thought about it lying in pieces on the floor. "It's not working. I was in the library reading."

Several seconds passed uneasily. He could see all the same old thoughts working in her, one after the other: the disappointment in him for leaving in the middle of class, her fears realized that he didn't have what it took to get into the world and make something of himself. His inability at the art of dedication, in which she excelled. "I wondered how you spent the day. Reading. That's good."

He shut the door. "Keep this locked, will you? That student downstairs doesn't even look up form his book when someone comes in. Who knows what kind of people you've got running around in here?"

"Funny how you use the word *student* to mean *asshole*."

"I'm just saying—"

"I know what you're saying."

"Lock it, Jo, okay?"

Tangled ringlets flipped back onto her face and she tugged them out of her mouth again. "All right."

She wavered between chastising him and being, possibly, nearly proud of him at the moment, he thought. He hoped she might at least respect the way he'd held to his own ethics, if that was what it had been. He tried not to consider the possibility that she'd been totally humiliated by his actions. She must've thought that Yokver would fail him now, and failure in all its forms terrified her.

"And so?" he asked.

"I'm not sure, Cal."

Another pause. The pregnant pauses were getting longer, and breeding what into their lives? She gave him this grimace, making a face like she was about to sneeze.

"Tell me what you're thinking, Jodi."

"It's not what I'm thinking, it's what you've been thinking about lately. Since before Christmas, and maybe a lot longer, I don't know. You've never said."

Okay, so they were into it.

She sat at her desk chair, arms and knees crossed as if to ward off blows. "I'm sorry I asked you to sign up for that damn course, but I thought we might enjoy taking it together."

"I wanted to take it. I thought it would be an easy grade." Melissa Lea had said that should've been the tip-off, and he'd fallen for the trap too.

"It's not hard to recognize you're completely infuriated with the man, and with everybody else lately, so far as I can see." She snorted, a rough and ugly sound, a sound her mother made all the time when she was about halfway into the gin bottle. "Part of that has to do with what happened over the winter vacation, and some with my parents, but not everything."

"No," he admitted.

"And I suppose I got on your nerves by not following you out of class this morning?"

A tightening in his chest urged him not to tell the truth, but he couldn't help himself. He could rarely help himself. "Of course it did. I wanted you to be on my side, instead of siding against me."

"Go on."

"But I—" He stifled his sentence, knowing he'd already made an extremely bad mistake. Stupid to have started the statement that way. Talking about her siding against him sounded so shamefully paranoid, like a schizophrenic yelling about the neighborhood dogs telling him to shoot up a WalMart, wearing tinfoil on his head to keep out alien signals from Neptune.

Her face folded in and she put that gaze on him, the one that showed absolutely nothing, as though she were actually examining a slide under a microscope, a cross section of a corpse's bowels.

"But?" she asked.

Caleb said nothing.

So she continued for him. "But you know how much I care about my grades, and you realize that if I had run out of there I would've taken a hit the same way you're going to now. You've undoubtedly failed the course."

No, he hadn't.

"Which would have wrecked my GPA in the same fashion that yours is effectively ruined. But you don't care. This is just playtime for you, all these years at school."

She didn't understand, and he couldn't explain it to her. He hadn't failed the course. Yok-ver would never demean himself that way. Giving Cal an A would be his way of putting the screws to him, teaching him yet another life lesson, like patting the patsy on the back after he gets the pie in his face. She would never believe it; she'd lived too long with the gold stars. Jodi would probably get shunted to a B, just so the Yok could show Cal how ethereal it all was, how little the degree meant in the grand design.

But he couldn't tell her that.

"And I care about such things and you don't," she said. "You're too comfortable in school."

"Hm."

"And you still wanted me to follow you."

"Yes," he said, giving a half-shrug. He could still be honest with her about these sorts of things, if she kept on asking.

"You want everything."

He sighed, but it didn't feel nearly as good as humming against Lady Dean's mink. "Everyone wants everything."

"Oh, that's goddamn original."

"Be that as it may—"

Another token moment of exaggerated silence, a sort of shadowboxing before the bout.

"A girl blew hell out of there right after you did," Jodi said, pulling a can of soda from the cube fridge. She emptied it in four gulps and tossed it in the garbage. The arching motion of her arm appeared extremely slow, her careful search for words affecting everything around them. "I saw that she winked at you when you started to brawl with Yokver. She's very pretty."

He told the truth. "I hadn't noticed."

"I wonder if she left because she hates Professor Yokver or because she likes you. What do you think?"

Cal stared at Jodi's dimples without his usual squint, surprised that she looked so different then, so out of focus. One of them was fading out of view. It was too late for her to try to act jealous; she knew he'd never cheat. She held out her hand to him, and he moved forward to sit with her, arm draped loosely around her shoulders.

He said, "I'm not even sure what we're talking about anymore."

"Even though we don't always see eye-to-eye anymore, or hardly ever, I still want you to know that I'm always behind you, in everything. It doesn't even matter that you've been lying to me. I accept that. It's a part of what we have."

Slithery panic rose to his scalp. Now they were off in another direction. "Jodi, for Christ's sake, don't say it that way."

"Do you understand?" She tugged on his knuckles, tenderly touching his wrist and taking his hand between hers. "It's important you believe me when I say I don't hold that against you, and you can't hold it against yourself."

"Jodi," he began and let it go for a while, unsure what to reveal beyond her name. The sorceress Circe stood to one side of him, and someone else, much angrier, stood on the other side. "Uhm . . ."

"Shhh, no more."

"Maybe it would be better if we got some things out in the open." He didn't really believe it, but maybe just the offer of it would help.

Snowfall had shifted to a blizzard, drawing impressionistic art on the windows. He watched it for a while, the crystals recomposing behind the gray steam of their breath on the inside glass. Streams of snowflakes burst against the pane like white flames: bizarre and vengeful.

"And maybe it wouldn't." Jodi pressed her fingers against his lips. "Shhh, Caleb Prentiss, I love you. I can accept what will never be between us. You are a darkly brooding man, filled with odd mysteries you'll never solve, and that's the way it should be."

"You make it sound perfectly frivolous."

"Sometimes that's the truth. It's one of the reasons I've always been so attracted to you."

"Why?" he asked. Sometimes you wanted poetry and sometimes you just wanted to get a goddamn straight answer. Was she being as evasive as he thought? Perhaps they were talking about love, or hate. There was no point describing it, in getting to a solution.

She kissed his chin and shushed him again. The shushing was starting to piss him off. "There's something inside you that's fascinating and intoxicating, that scratches up against my sensitive spots like your beard stubble, like your hands. I've never asked you, have I?"

About what? About nothing. "No."

"When you went on your binges . . . when you nearly broke your legs . . . when you disappear for hours on end, claiming to be reading books. I'm aware you're playing out another side of yourself I don't comprehend."

You and me both, baby. "Don't keep putting it into words."

She pushed him down on the bed, palms against his chest. Jodi, too, played out a side of herself that, for his life, Cal couldn't embrace. "Yokver knows it too," she said. "So do the dean and your other professors. Don't you see that's why they toy with you so much, because they respect you? It's on account of the fact that you're so much like them."

"Now you're just being mean," he said.

He tried to sit up, but she held him to the

sheets. Damn, she had some real muscle to her. And she had a piece of the truth now too, more than he'd expected, but he didn't know what to make of that tone of voice. She was being evasive by getting right up into his face. It was a good trick, and it worked.

Jodi opened his shirt and kissed his chest, carelessly and slow; she'd been more horny in the past couple of months than at any other time since he'd known her. "It makes perfect sense, Cal. A hunter doesn't go after woodchucks. He wants what gives him a challenge."

"I don't get the analogy."

"Yes, you do, my love. Keep yourself safe. Stay out of the forest. Out of the jungle."

He sniffed her breath to see if there was a hint of liquor or grass. He only smelled himself, which was bad enough. "Tonight's the dean's party. Is that what you're talking about?"

She tensed, or maybe he did, at the sharpness of his own timbre right then. Nervous energy swarmed them both, and he couldn't tell if he was aroused or angry, or if she was either.

"Who told you about that?" she asked.

"Why would you ask me that?" This time he grabbed her wrists and hauled her forward into his lap. They pinned each other on the bed. At another time this would have been a lot of fun. "Who told *you* about it?"

"Everyone heard."

"No. If I hadn't tripped over him and his wife out there, I still wouldn't know anything about it."

"So? Is that so bad?"

"Somebody's keeping secrets." He'd never told her about the murder in his room, and she'd never found out. He couldn't keep his mind on any single track of thought. Her nipples hardened, their dark outlines distinct against her blouse. "Why didn't you tell me, Jodi?" The angle of her breasts was perfect in this light, and he saw the soft down of her cleavage. He pressed his face to it and went, "Hmmm."

"Don't rise after their bait," she told him. Her canines crept over her bottom lip. The mischievous smile was so unlike her that he sought out the freckles, beauty marks, and scars to reassure him of just who he was now facing. His mouth started to go dry. "Teach me, Cal."

"Teach you what?"

"Teach me. Forgive me."

The cold sweat coursed down his forehead. "Forgive you for what, Jo?"

"Please."

He tried to speak and nothing came out. She jammed her tongue into his mouth and then pulled away, then came after him again. "You're being eaten," she said, ravenously. He almost didn't recognize the voice, it was so much like her mother's. "Eaten alive." She slid down his belly, licking and nibbling, hands working. She flashed her tongue.

He figured she was right, and as he fell over onto Jodi, drawn into the wet and meaty crevices, his sister spit those same garbled words that meant nothing when she died, and even less now.

Forgive me.

Chapter Seven

Maybe he did forgive her, in his nightmares, where he could afford to do so.

Jodi snored and mumbled softly in her sleep, sounding like Fruggy Fred. She blew knotted strands of hair from in front of her nose. What had once been love and lust had now become lust, love, and a newly added dimension of love, a mislaid or mismanaged side of devotion. It would've been a lot smarter to have just ended it, but who can ever do the smart thing when it needs to be done? Some of her tenderness had been put down beside his futility, a sacrifice made to his impiety, he guessed. Cal felt a stinging guilt about that. Traps of double-talk sweet nothings and other lovers' romantic nonsense didn't move in synch with the reality they shared.

The bells rang three times.

Only three o'clock in the afternoon, and yet most of his life seemed to have been lived out today. Replayed over and again as he watched, waited, and lingered. Like his sister, he couldn't quite accept what the world had to offer. Maybe he should work with rats. Be a rat catcher and drive around in a van full of poison, watching them rutting around in the dead. Or become a rat wrangler out in Hollywood, working on the Universal back lots. Or just be a rat *breeder*. Funny to think about it, that he still followed in the same kind of track as her, despite all the warnings. His moods, as hers had been, were mercurial and retrograde. No wonder she'd called him into the bathroom.

He thumped his head twice on the pillows, hoping to beat those snakes out. The agitated movement roused Jodi. She looked up at him, smiled, and sleepily whispered, "Hey."

"Hey there yourself."

Cal kept watch until he was certain she wasn't going to drop off again, smoothing the back of his hand along her cheeks, tickling the back of her ears until she giggled. It could still be sweet, thank God. His fingers circulated over the tiny gutters of scars, wiping lashes out of her eyes and connecting the red marks where he'd nipped her with his teeth. Shadows of swaying snowflakes darkened her belly. He refashioned the lines of her face until he once again saw that first version of Sylvia Campbell he'd originally created.

His throat constricted when he realized what he was doing. His loving gaze snapped with a nearly audible twang.

"Who told you about the dean's party?" he said.

"Do we have to talk about this now? Even after making love you circle back to that."

"I'm not circling."

"You are circling."

"Okay, so I'm circling. So tell me."

"And what if I don't want to talk about it?" she said. She couldn't keep the nyah-nyah dare out of her voice, the tinge of a threat.

"Why didn't you tell me?"

"Stop, Cal, please . . ."

"Aren't we going to go together?"

"You never let up, do you? You've always got to push!" With her mouth compressed into a bluish-white lipless line, she regarded him for a full minute. It was maybe the longest minute of his life. There was no reason for this. "Why is it that you get so screwedup about such inconsequential things?"

123

"Inconse . . . ?"

"Trivialities! Why are you either completely reckless or totally unnerved?"

"Is that really what I am?" he asked.

Yes, that sounded about right. He drew away and smacked his shoulder into one of her framed Robert Doiseneau posters hanging beside the bed: '50s Paris rocked back and forth, indistinct darkened figures walking on cobblestones tilted and swung like the hanging man.

"Yes!"

"Why don't you simply answer me, Jo?"

Her hands worked the sheets. "I don't remember. Rose maybe. I think she said she and Willy were invited."

"Them too? Then how come I wasn't?"

"You were! You are!"

"But—"

A slamming knock at the door resounded in the room. Both of them jumped under the sheets, jerking away from each other. Jodi quickly dressed and tried to unsnarl her hair as Cal threw on his pants.

Another fierce pounding. The whole door shook in its frame, like they were out there really throwing their shoulder into it now. Somebody wanted in badly. Jodi went to answer and Cal came close to shouting for her to stop. That student downstairs could've let in anybody. The killer returned to finish cutting up everybody who slept in that bed.

Rose stood in the hallway crying uncontrollably, covered in snow, her mouth fluttering, eyes rolling insanely, all kinds of weird colors in her face. Cal held back an *oh, shit*. She bustled past Jodi and rushed inside, a hawk descending on a field mouse, hurtling toward him. Cal knew what it was about. Open relationship, his ass.

Goddamn Willy and that macho bullshit about never letting it get too serious, telling Cal that they could share Rose, knowing her better but blinded by his libido. Caleb couldn't decide if he should jump out the window or not. Only three stories. Go to Plan B if there happened to be one. Ah, fuck, there wasn't.

Look at her; why didn't Willy just break a few of her ribs instead. She stopped a foot away from him and stared through Cal's pupils and went digging into his brain. Her expression shifted across the entire spectrum: full of horror, humiliation, revulsion, and pain, all of it flung in every direction. He would've felt exactly the same way. He cringed, a boy about to be beaten to death and pretty much deserving it. Her nail polish flaked to the floor as she scraped her fingernails together, *skrt, skrt, skrt, skrt*, sharpening them for his eyes. That action alone proved menacing enough. He backed up a couple more steps. People had been known to survive three-story falls.

The moment kept expanding, swallowing them. Rose's face appeared hard as stone, bone white and blue from the cold; the ice crystals in her hair hadn't even had time to melt yet. She'd run across the quad through the blizzard without a coat on. The edges of her eyebrows were slick with sweat, smeared makeup, and tears. Mascara had been brushed all over her forehead and across her ears, so that she had the wild bandit look of a rabid raccoon.

"I have to talk to you," Rose sobbed. "And I want the truth."

He managed to say, "Sure."

"Who is he with, Cal? I've had my suspicions, but now I know for sure." Steam rose from her face in arching wisps. "Please, no matter what kind of promises you made, don't lie to me now. I never thought you were even capable of it! Tell me, tell me, please." She kneeled before him, wet and trembling, as frayed as a leather strop about to snap in half. He winced, his heart lurching to the left like it was trying to yank him the hell out of there. He fell back a step, and then another, until he was nearly pressed against the window. "Please."

"I don't know, Rose."

She gritted her teeth and snorted, lanky brown curls dripping with the melting snow, rheumy eyes sticky with cream. "You're my friend." She took his hand and attempted to bring it to her chest, slowly, too slowly, so that the action became somehow intimate. It should've been anything but that. She stopped and turned his hand over, staring at his palm as though reading both of their futures there. What'd she see?

"Yes, I am."

In one terrifying instant she quit crying, as if a blade had come down and severed her neck. He tried to pull his hand back and she struggled to hold on. "You've been my friend since we first met for orientation, Cal. You made me laugh and stay when all I wanted to do was run home to my parents. You're a larger part of my life than you'll ever know, and even though we haven't always gotten along, I love you, and I need you to help me right now."

From across the room he saw one awful shudder after another strike down Jodi's spine. "I don't know," he said.

"Don't lie!"

"I'm not."

He kept trying to get his hand back and she wouldn't let it go. She tugged harder and harder until he thought his arm might come out of its socket. "He tells you things, Cal, I understand that, it's supposed to just be between you guys. But you're my friend too."

"I am, Rose, I—"

Jesus, God, all the makeup running into a flood of colors, as if she'd had her face smashed in. "It feels like I'm dying; he couldn't have made it worse if he'd slit my throat!"

Enough with the murdered women. "I swear, Rose, I don't know."

"Please!" she wailed, a long plaintive, infantile whine. He finally managed to get his hand back and now he wanted to cover his ears. "I'm not an idiot!" As her hate drained away, so did his, until, out of their element, there was nothing left to do. He reached and caressed her cheek, like that might actually do something.

"He doesn't tell me anything like that." It sounded completely inane, but there was no other way to do it.

"But—"

"I'm telling you the truth, Rose." Wishing he had something more intelligent or sincere to say, he reached and found his shoes and shirt and put them on. Willy, the son of a bitch, ought to be here to see what he'd done and clean up after his own macho messes.

"You're a fucking goddamn piece of shit liar," Rose hissed. "And you always have been."

No, he thought, not always.

"Go on, run. Get out of here. Get out of my sight."

He left her kneeling there and grabbed his coat. Jodi moved out of the doorway and allowed Cal just enough clearance to leave, evading the slant of his chin because she thought he might try to kiss her.

Incomprehensible sounds followed him down three flights of stairs and past the front desk. The kid doing his calculus didn't look up as Cal snatched his ID and plunged into the blizzard.

Without destination, he twisted in the freeze, snow whipping into his eyes and burning like the grit the devil winds had shoveled over him during Christmas vacation. For fifteen minutes he followed other footprints across the nearly indistinguishable trails across the quad.

Before he knew he was even inside a building he was abruptly walking down the narrow hallways of the radio station, stamping snow off his shoes and heading for the broadcasting booth of KLAP.

Cal wasn't sure whether he should be here. But it was better to sit in silence with Fruggy Fred than to stew alone in his room, the library, out in the storm, or hunting around for Willy.

He'd never even found out how Rose had discovered Willy was cheating on her.

Speakers inside the station blared "Alice's Restaurant." Arlo Guthrie's reedy voice set the audience to giggling with his twenty-five-minute long comic tale of war and woe, hippiedom and garbage dump blues.

Shishka Bob, hunkered in the corner searching through a hundred worn album covers and CD cases, glanced up. That bright pink bald spot shimmered, his scraggly mustache quivering when he spoke. "Hey, Frosty, I thought you couldn't move without your magic hat."

Cal caught sight of his reflection in the mirror behind the racks where Bob crouched. His hair and jacket were totally white, his face scarlet from windburn. He checked out his hair from different angles, knowing that was what he was going to look like soon, going gray way too early.

"Haven't seen you and Willy-boy around for a while," Bob said. "What's been happening?"

"Would you believe we've been working hard?"

"Only if you've been volunteering at orphanages as well, giving a pint of blood every three months, and have collected three tons of aluminum foil for the annual recycling drive."

"You're a kind soul."

Shishka Bob shrugged. "Do you have any idea what album Dylan's 'Lily, Rosemary, and the Jack of Hearts' is on?' "

"Highway Sixty-one?"

"No, I checked that. What brings you around this early?'

"Fruggy Fred on yet?"

"Yeah, zonked on the couch as always. He's got about another five minutes to shake himself awake before Arlo brings it to a close."

"Think he'll make it?"

Bob glanced up, poised on becoming extremely serious. "We both know that he always does."

Caleb nodded. "When do you go on?"

"At four." Bob checked his watch. "Precisely fifteen minutes. That gives you ten minutes to screw around on the air if you want to. I disavow any knowledge of your actions." He flipped over the CD of Bob Dylan's *Blood on the Tracks*. "Ah-ha. There's the bastard. Too bad I've got to play the latest campus hit. Some English guy trying hard to merge Skinny Puppy with Nine-Inch Nails and Harvey Danger. Wish they'd let me get away with tossing some true classics in on occasion."

Cal threw his coat across the room at the coatrack, missed, and stepped into the broadcasting booth.

There lay Fruggy Fred in his glorious somnolence—too damn bizarre and beautiful, with ivory flesh hanging low over the cushions of the cot where he slept.

He had on an ill-fitting hockey jersey that had been hiked up to his belly button, the long pink stretch marks on his belly painfully clear. People mistook him for lazy or clinically depressed, but Cal knew Fruggy was the most dedicated and well-disciplined man he'd ever met. Others might guess that Willy truly was the obsessive one, with the ridges of his sinews cut into a physical masterpiece, and they'd be right about some of it but wrong about the rest. There was power in a reality strike.

It was Fruggy Fred who allowed his muscles to atrophy, who gave up his waking life trying to untie the Freudian-Gordian knot of his nightmare symbols, always in search of unknown psycho-theology in the recesses of his unconscious mind. Cal had no idea what had driven him so decisively onto this course of active inaction, or what it was he'd already found or hoped to achieve. Jodi vehemently hated Fruggy. It would well up inside her and sharpen the planes of her face, raise her upper lip in a sneer of revulsion for what she believed to be inherent sloth. Part of it was jealousy, Cal thought: Fruggy's family was wealthy, and he could afford to get an incomplete or even fail a course without it affecting his future. He'd eventually take over his father's software business—either that or sell it and be set for the rest of his life, such as it were. Even so, Fruggy made the dean's list every year, straight A's all the time.

Caleb loved him.

Their relationship was one based on total and pure acceptance, unadulterated by judgment, ethical or otherwise. Fruggy's silence was often the only thing he could ally himself with. Sitting here beside that sleeping bulk was like being before the graves of loved ones who died before you could say how much you loved them. Fruggy Fred's REM flickering eyes would put you at ease.

It was the same way you trusted the dead to keep your secrets. Fruggy listened, yet consciously did not *know*. That was Cal's theory, anyway. Pillows squeezed between his knees leaked feathers into the air whenever he twisted with a particularly powerful vision.

This wasn't inertia, it was action.

Cal sat at the console, put on the headphones and fiddled with the control board, refamiliarizing himself. "Alice's Restaurant" came to a close and Fruggy Fred groaned and began to sit up.

"Relax," Cal said. "I've got it."

Fruggy blinked wearily and fell back onto the cushions with a huff.

Hunching forward to the boom, Cal couldn't think of anything witty to say for an intro. He merely ID'ed Joy Division's "Love Will Tear Us Apart" and cued the disc. "An oldie but a goodie," he said. He set up the second CD player with Zenith Brite's "I'll Never Write." He thought there was a line in there about fuses that he wanted to hear again.

The windowless room grew warmer; about the same size as the storage room, the cozy, well-lit milieu here gave the place a different feel. He almost missed the chill of the storage room. Cal rubbed his eyes until he saw red stars. "What's the answer?" he whispered.

Fruggy Fred sighed and murmured.

Hm. Cal spun casually in his seat, trying not to make excessive noise. If you were very careful, you might be able to hold a conversation with Fruggy in his somnambulistic state. He waited.

"What was that?" Cal asked, calm and patient, drawing out his words the way they'd sound in a dream.

"It's real," said Fruggy Fred in his sleep.

"What is?"

"The place."

"Which?"

"Hell," Fruggy said. By the end of the song he'd added, "Heaven. Death." His breathing became even more shallow and rapid. Tongue lolling, his eyes battered the undersides of his eyelids. "Where we're kept."

Cal slid back in the chair and cued the Zenith Brite song. "You're not telling me anything I don't already know."

"They're all around us," Fruggy whispered.

"You're right."

"Even now."

"Yes."

"All of them."

"Can you find her, Fruggy?"

Fruggy Fred's brow knitted, mouth forming an *O*, his breathing growing more excited with nightmare.

"Can you find Sylvia Campbell?" Cal asked.

Perhaps the name she'd given was a fake as well. But he was thinking so hard about her life and death now, so focused, that he'd slash through the lie. He believed, like the Navajo, that names held power and could bring the dead back, even if only in your thoughts.

Sy. C.

Skinwalkers, the Navajo called their witches. Circe, the sorceress. She, or someone—perhaps his sister—hesitated for an instant and then moved forward and came closer to him.

"Can you tell me what she's dreaming? Ask her, Fruggy. Ask her who did this to her."

Fruggy nodded eagerly.

Zenith sang the opening stanza *a cappella*, humming with a growl and lilt that plucked at your guts.

And every time you try to get near
I take it as an attack
Your letters from the dark don't even come
        close
to the mark
and you're way too inane for my pain
You'll never guess the secrets of my deep-red
        success
until you stop your dull aching
and blow your own fuse
A man like you has got nothing left to lose
it's all black
'cause no matter how much you need me
you'll never totally bleed me
and I'll never write you back.

Fruggy groaned softly, air whistling out of him. He sniffled and muttered more solemn warnings. "Don't . . . Cal, don't . . ."

"What?"

"Don't . . . !"

"We're all nuts," Caleb said, secure in the knowledge.

Twitching violently, Fruggy's fist brushed against Cal, reaching. He was sobbing in his sleep now, tears coursing down his face. He caught the front of Cal's shirt and desperately pulled him closer.

Fruggy Fred whimpered, *"Circe. She'll be at the party."*

Part Two

Dream of a Shadow

Chapter Eight

He stumbled into the blizzard heading for the Avenue.

By the time he got there it was getting dark and the plows were sanding and clearing the streets. He got onto the downtown bus. Half an hour later he got off at the corner two blocks from the Buzzed Owl, a strip joint where most of the girls were younger than him.

It was only five but that was late enough for the action to be going strong, especially when the weather was this bad. Willy virtually owned a seat at the bar, always sitting around grinning widely at the leather and lace, slack-jawed in front of the blonde with the thirty-eight-inch bust with pigtails, holding a whip, something to be said for the virgin whore.

Beyond the Avenue, north of the Owl, you could just make out a faint glow of flickering candles lighting the stained-glass windows of Saint Ignatius. Cal noted the years his sister had devoted to that faith, and all the other time she'd given to the nailed man, and wondered where the fracture had started. If she'd begun to rot because of that green van, or if the sickness had always been there in the chromosomes.

He hoped Christ could forgive her, or that she could forgive God, because he could never do either.

Doorway blocked by love beads hanging to the floor, the place reeked of stale beer and marijuana. The stink hit him like a bat and he almost went over. It took a while to get used to. He slipped through the beads into the Buzzed Owl. Obscurity meant security. He scanned for Willy but couldn't spot him among the throng of shadows. His hands shook as he reached for his wallet. He never thought he'd say it, but he needed a drink badly. It was time to binge.

The bouncer could have parked a Mazda in his navel if only there wasn't so much lint jammed inside from his HARLEY RULES T-shirt. His hairy beer belly hung naked over his belt.

The buckle was actually a tiny knife he could pull if things ever got too critical in here. He checked Cal's university ID and gave the usual snigger that slobbish bouncers gave when they saw he was a college boy. It was part of the anonymity factor, safe and secure, though you might have a tendency to start saying "Yup" and dropping the *g* off your *ing* endings in a place like this. Cal took his identification back, trying hard to keep his shaky grip on his wallet. The bouncer stood aside with a reluctant shrug and let him pass.

The jukebox pumped out the opening bass licks of a Nocturnal Emission tune, wooden floor vibrating. The thrum beat through his chest and up into his throat. Out of the corner of his eye he spotted dollar bills waving in the smoky air. Peripheral vision picked up the edges of dancers doing their thing, languorous and vicious, to the beat, but he beelined for the bar against the far wall.

A waitress zipped over to him before the bartender at the other end had a chance to move from her stool, both of them looking for his tip, both of them just as seductive as the dancers on the stage. Probably more so, leaving something to the imagination. A thick trail of smoke wafted after her as she moved sideways along the length of the bar and sidled up too close to

Tom Piccirilli

him, making him wince. Speed became an urgency in strip joints, everybody moving in for the kill.

Her lips were pulpy and thick with a little too much waxy cherry lipstick, face so full of eyeliner that she looked like an Egyptian using ashes and kohl to keep the dead out of her eyes. Maybe she knew something he didn't. "Hey there, honey bun, now what can I getcha?"

"Double shot of whiskey boilermaker."

"Bad day at school, huh?" she asked, with an extra digging twist that made it sound like grade school, little boy blue wearing his shiny shoes, carrying his lunchbox, practicing for a spelling bee, cowlick slicked down and Mama's kiss fresh on his cheek. His fingers were already twitching. It got like this sometimes, when the need was on him. She shuttled around the other side of the bar and made him the drink herself. She handed him a double shot of Four Roses and a mug of tap beer. "Here ya go." She had a nice smile, the kind you wanted to trust but never would. "You want a match so you can light it, hon?"

"No thanks." Cal dumped the shot in the mug and guzzled the drink before the beer had even begun to foam. It was stupid, acting this way in front of her, but he couldn't help himself.

She crooked her head the way a dog will at a

144

weird sound. "That kind of defeats the purpose of having a boilermaker, don't it?" she asked. "After all, it's supposed to boil."

"I think the purpose is that it's supposed to get you drunk."

"And that's all you're after, huh? Okay then . . . another?"

"Yup."

"Fail a big test, did ya?" Those words whispered under her breath, slightly sarcastic but not in a particularly bitter way, just loud enough to be heard. She kept smiling, kept staring into his eyes with interest. That took the sharpness from it. He liked what the Egyptian makeup did for her. "You didn't even pause to take a gander at the girls."

Gander. He had never said the word *gander* in his entire life.

"I've only got eyes for you, lil darlin'."

"Oh, you sweet thang."

Those dark eyes batted at him, knowing it was a game now, and she was already sort of sick of it. If you showed any interest at all they backed the fuck right off. She handed him his drinks, and this time he didn't bother to shoot them together. He gulped the whiskey and followed it with a long draw of the beer, draining the mug and letting the last few drops swirl around in his mouth before sucking them down, the way Jodi's mother did it.

"Another?" Cal said, realizing he was pushing it too quickly, and that the bouncer was watching too. He thought of all the mirrors in the place shattering, the furniture wheeling through the air and splintering, girls laughing and shrieking and running naked into the snow. "Please."

She was thinking the same thing. "Sure, but then why don't you turn around and help yourself to watchin' the girls for a while so you can take a few deep breaths, okay, sweetie?"

"Yup, it's a deal."

For the last drink he allowed her to light a match and set the whiskey on fire before dropping it into the beer and letting it foam over. Yippee, a boilermaker. He was surprised to see that she really did get some kind of kick out of watching him down it that way. He guzzled, letting the last mouthful settle against his tongue so that the liquor took out his taste buds. He dropped a twenty on the bar and swung around in his seat, and wandered closer to the tables at the foot of the stage.

Strobes and dimly blinking neon lights threw out flashes of sweaty sexuality into the darkness, along with glints of wet black hair. Torrid and sultry shadows glided on the walls, girls fitting themselves against the brace poles, straddling and humping as they coldly stroked up and down and up, jerking back and forth. It bothered him somewhat to realize that he had actually missed this. The gloom was split with a moment of bright white, then a couple of kicks of orange before going black. No way to tell just how many girls there were with the lights flickering so wickedly, dancers appearing to move in mechanical stop-and-go motions, bodies twisting as they flung themselves across the stage, guys entranced, tits bouncing, chicks slinking over there, now here, there against other men, the music still driving.

They'd get a nice tip for some lesbo action and the girls worked it out whenever they could, French kissing each other but looking kind of bored, and yet still licking nipples, sucking tongue like cock, putting just enough effort into it to work. It still drove all the guys insane.

High heels caused popping static sparks on the carpet, bursts of blue and yellow lighting up their ankles. You couldn't get much more than a peek at the garters flashing by so fast, a voluptuous leg kicked high over a blond head, there were a few pierced nipples, lots of tight asses. Creamy movements, gliding and spinning, ribs showing as they cut to the corners to sniff some coke.

You could see the welts and bruises too, and the yellowed bite marks; time became greased in just how you liked it, sex exalted as it should be, the minutes stretching and peeling further away. Listening to the deep breaths of ghosts, the living catcalls, the nasty *tsks* when somebody nursed a beer. They didn't take any shit, this was a business, you want to put a nipple on that beer then get the fuck out. Two oiled girls struggled to keep standing while clenched in a not entirely faked writhing drunken lick fest; the money floated toward their feet. They went down to their knees, then over onto their backs. It brought roars before they finally quit pushing it. Flurries of wild teased hair lifted even farther into the air, and from the floor came the hooting of boys and old men as they shouted and laughed like killers striking the mark.

The strobes blinked off and the houselights burned bright in one brutal moment of clarity that made Caleb dizzy. It took a minute to get used to it as he took in the anemia of everyone's skin, the bareness of the room, the lack of his own pity.

And Willy over at a table.

Sitting at the end of the first row with a line of six empty beer bottles in front of him, kicked back in a chair staring up at the stage where a girl hoochie-cooed in front of him, bobbing her breasts in his face.

Cal stood and stared.

He drew the icy sweat off his throat with the back of his hand.

"Oh my Christ," he said.

It was Candida Celeste dancing up there. Cheerleader, owner of his one-time freshman heart, lovely lady piece of work who tangled feet with no-neck bruiser types who didn't know what a jihad was, and she liked to yuk it up with the Yok. She was a goddess returned to the earth. Cal almost laughed, but forgot how to the second he opened his mouth.

Reflections made it seem that she and Willy twisted and moved in contortions everywhere as she draped herself over him, like they were making love or murdering one another. Red light washed up her arms as she wove them serpent style above her head, taking it slow, performing an impromptu belly dance. Willy drank his beer and gradually slipped a dollar into the front of her G-string, crowding her, pressing further, trying to get his finger deep inside there too, going after the pink. She smiled and backed away, taking the buck.

They played the game well, like old friends forecasting each other's moves. They had done this many times before. Caleb never suspected

she was a stripper, although there was no reason not to think so. All those months of agonized freshman infatuation, and now here she
stood naked before him, selling the scenes that
had consumed him four years ago. But why
hadn't Willy ever told him?

He ordered another boilermaker, from the
bartender this time, and sucked it down without realizing how jittery he was in the guts and
yet how steady his hands were. That wasn't the
way it should've been. He sat beside Willy, directly at eye level with Candida Celeste's slim
ankles, tiny chains tinkling together there.

"Her stage name is Cool Breeze," Willy told
him.

"Of course it is," Cal said.

Sweat slipped down his spine, and he could
see salt trails along her cleavage. Jesus, why
hadn't anybody ever told him about this? She
glanced at him and read his mind, those knowing eyes making him feel much more naked
than her. A different kind of smile crawled
across her face, one that was frightening, kind
of, but erotic and conquering. She'd always
have something over him, and he'd never be
able to find out what it was, or loosen its hold.

Staring directly into his eyes, bending all the
way over until she clutched her ankles, she
shook her ass in a deliberate shimmy until his

nose grazed her inner thighs. The beauty marks on her tits fascinated him, large brown aureola so streaked with sweat they looked buttered, and they reminded him of his sister's wet breasts in the blood-filled tub.

"Hi, Calvin," she said with a moan, going for his soft belly. "About time you came to see me. I was starting to think you were never going to show."

He sucked air through his teeth until his tongue dried. He felt as if he hadn't taken a breath in twenty-five minutes. She whirled and gave him a hard grin, her smile so much more natural than he remembered. "I've been waiting for you, Calvin." Cooing cut short, she gave a deeply erotic cackle.

Rose's agonized cries tried to bob around him again, but the surface tension was too great. She couldn't get all the way through to him now. He turned to Willy and then turned back. Even with Jodi's love holding him firmly in place, the fantasies jarred free inside him, watching Candida Celeste as she floated down the stage now, talking with all those other men. Each time she arched ever so slightly to gaze back at him, knowing what it was doing to him especially. She moved and began grinding against the brace pole as Skitch & Stich's "Parts of Your Heart" kicked on:

The machine's running with ease
but I can't afford to please her
much longer
Well-oiled box springs and baths
only slow the aftermath
I wish my credit was stronger
Winter white diamonds reflect perfect steel
    gray
Between the bag ladies and bad boys there's
    nothing left to say
The forty-fifth floor lost another anemic
    today
and the sucker only missed me by inches

She stuck the tip of her tongue out from between her teeth, and Willy pursed his lips and
licked them at her. Cal saw a ton of loose cash
down on the table and had no idea where Willy
had gotten the money from. He seemed a part
of the show, a paid performer, unreal in his own
design. Caleb couldn't concentrate, the alcohol
finally having some effect.

Willy called the waitress over, smiled his
most sincere smile, and ordered another round.
She asked him something and he answered,
"Yup." Jo's voice tuned in and out. Candida returned and slung herself over the table. She
grabbed for Cal's crotch, searching for the best
compliment he could give her.

"Oh my, baby, do you want to use that on me?" she asked, laughing as she whirled away.

Other men flocked to her feet. Willy gave a loud hoot. Cal had another shot and drank Willy's beer and his own. His muscles locked and the glacial rage crawled out of the back of his skull and sick jealousy made him tremble. Someone turned the music up. The lyrics weren't quite lyrics anymore, just a slice of the moment, as she kneeled on another table and slowly humped against each of the bland figures, to the backbeat.

Cocaine deals in my wheels make them roll
    slower
Bundled baby cuts me off in his stroller
His mother didn't bother to signal
Hurricane hums and slides with the slush
as the Pope-mobile screams by in a rush
while the baby snaps his rattle looking regal
Milkman's in my bed, my wife she's
    shouting loud
Outside our apartment I see smiles in the
    crowd
My cat's tossed its kittens, my cattle threw a
    cow
and the sucker only missed me by inches.

Candida Celeste stepped past the other men and returned to her place in front of Cal, slinky and sweaty, bowing to blow chilly streams of breath in his face. It felt so good that he actually fucking *quivered*, the freshman in him and every other part too. Going out of control with lust and the memories of lust. Willy clapped him on the back and whispered, "Relax, you're too tense."

Cal wanted to take a lead pipe to him. Cal shook like a bow pulled way too taut. Willy kept laughing, forever smooth and comfortable in his needs, assured of his ability to meet them. He always went after differences—taller, tanner, thinner, hipper, more muscular, anything different. It was why he had become a part of this game, and played it by rote, already bored to death. Willy knew Candida's body the way he knew Rose's, just like the way he knew his own. No wonder Willy had never told him—he wanted to save Cal from this resolution.

Candida Celeste made faces in the night at the men, dollars nudged under her garters like dozens of Washington, Lincoln, and Jackson miniatures climbing her legs, seeking a hospice against her skin. "Take out your wallet and maybe I'll let you have a look at some of the pink," she told him.

"Uhm."

"Wouldn't you like that, Calvin?" He almost wished it was his name. Through the drunken dimness he'd caught a hint of another angle to the world.

> Lucifer drops off his laundry, and I
> > ain't got no bleach
> There's dolphins in the bathtub, my
> > kid's at the beach
> Lessons are ludicrous, there's nothing
> > left to teach
> But the world keeps on learnin' and
> > burnin'
> The forty-fifth floor won a new
> > anemic today
> and he cuddled his secretary and she
> > had nothing to say
> except that God and Mary are flinging
> > pitchforks in the hay
> and the sucker only missed me by
> > inches.

Cool Breeze stopped her sexy swaying.

She leaned forward and kneeled on their table, those legs parting slightly as her sweat slid over the arch of her muscles. She grabbed him by the chin, tugging him into a realm of ethereal intimacy, where the music, lights, Willy, and everything else all faded beyond the silhouette of her body, as her lips parted.

He swallowed and eased toward her.

The tip of her tongue exposed and moving. He waited, wide-eyed, as he saw the points of her shining teeth coming for him. Her smile didn't stop until it wasn't a smile anymore, tugged all the way up into a sneer. Hatred he'd seen up close a couple of hours ago—when Rose had seethed in his face—peered down at him again, pulling him nearer. It had followed him here. Even closer, until the overhead crimson beams shined directly on both their heads.

Cal witnessed the curl of her upper lip teased back over the canines, showing streams of black from a rotted back tooth, her cracked nostrils full of bleeding, tiny red lines from heavy cocaine use, as her brow furrowed and her mouth thinned.

The look of annoyance spiked her features. She looked like she wanted to cut his throat. Candida Celeste, this new version of her, shoved him away and said, "What is your problem, you asshole?"

He gawked and still didn't get it.

She said, "Do you think this is free?"

And there it was. In a humiliating flash he realized she'd grown tired of this tease and just wanted him to fork over the cash. This was a job, after all, and not an easy one. His face burned bright. He fumbled for his wallet, and stray fives and tens fell out over her gnarled toe-nails.

What was his problem? Cool Breeze squatted and snatched the bills off the carpet, the way his mother had plucked up dust bunnies, then stood and stalked to the other end of the row of tables, smiling and dancing once more. Willy sighed as her ass wriggled away.

"I didn't know you had a thing for her too," Caleb said.

"I don't. You do. At least you did, before you came in. What are you doing here, anyway?"

"Good question. I left two ladies in Jodi's room who are more than slightly miffed at me."

Willy didn't look up from his beer. Some of his money had scattered to the floor, but he didn't care enough to pick it up. "Too bad."

"One of them was crying hysterically. Would you care to reassess that whole load of shit about you and Rose not being serious?"

"It's not supposed to be."

"Oh," Cal said, "well, that's nice. Maybe you should have notified her of that fact."

"Don't preach, all right?"

Both of them kept to the same monotone. "I'm not."

"I know you are. Keep out of it."

Cal tried to take a drink from his empty mug. "It's hard to keep out of it when somebody comes banging on the door pleading and wailing uncontrollably because her heart is broken. I'm her friend."

"Hmm," Willy went.

"She said she feels as though she's been knifed, and I know how I'd react if it had been Jodi." He was on the verge of slurring his words. His stomach tumbled. "You lied to me."

"The fuck I did."

"Then what the hell do you call it?"

Willy flexed his shoulder muscles, the meat of his back carved and packed with power. "Hey, look, since the first day of the semester you've drifted around campus like a goddamn zombie. You don't talk about where you were or what you're doing or who you're doing it with." Nothing vindictive in his manner, just honesty and a show of concern.

"But—"

"You don't listen to me, or Rose, or Jodi, for that matter, or anybody else so far as I can see, and you're so out of it you wouldn't know who was hurting if they up and fucking died twice in your arms. So you can just cool it with the cry for my confession until you're ready to cough up some yourself."

"Me?" was all Caleb managed to say. He sounded about as stupid as he actually was. The echo of his own voice hung in the air like a dagger twirling, aimed and intractable. He hadn't been able to finish many sentences lately. "Look, you didn't have to sit there and face her. I—"

Willy didn't want to hear it and had already spun in his seat to watch the show again. He was smiling, totally back into the groove, bored but at least bored doing something he liked. Candida Celeste had finished going up the line and was now strutting back to the beginning.

You had to let go sometimes, until you figured out what the hell you were talking about. Cal got up and made his way to the door and shoved past the slob of a bouncer, who still sniggered at him the way all bouncers sniggered at college boys who couldn't handle a little too much fun.

The wind whistles screeched louder than the music, like rats in the subway. Cal rushed into the snow, where he might trade in his yups for yeses again. In the darkness it still felt as though he were falling over. He looked to the church as if expecting divine answers to all his hellish questions, but the flickering candlelit panes remained nearly hidden behind frost. He couldn't make up his mind as to whether God had failed him or he'd failed God. One of them ought to take responsibility.

Cal caught the bus. Leaning his cheek against

the window, he dozed for the hour it took to get back to campus, letting the whiskey do its thing. He hadn't had enough to really do him good, but at least he'd drunk the liquor quickly. Now the soothing numbness was bursting against him in waves. The hiss of the air brakes startled him awake, and while trying to clear the six-pound hair ball from his throat he made his way forward to exit.

A woman wearing a plastic kerchief had two bags of assorted secondhand romance novels stuck out in the middle of the aisle. She tugged them closer to her knees, trying to get them out of the way, with bronze god Fabio grinning bare-chested from several covers.

"Thanks," Cal muttered.

Someone screamed.

He wheeled, looking around for a murderer. More shrieks and shouts as the bus erupted with activity. People shifted in their seats, scrambling and struggling to get past one another. The emergency window clacked open and a skinny guy jumped out and hit the ground running. A girl followed, and somebody yelled to get a cop. The bus driver rolled his eyes, wondering what the hell was happening. The lady with the kerchief pointed at Caleb.

Blood continued spurting from the holes in his palms.

Chapter Nine

He whirled, knowing death.

Foolishly, he listened to the squeaks he made as he dragged his wet fists along the shining metal handrails, leaving behind red trails. The lady in the kerchief with the romance novels kept pointing, silent and bloated and accusing. Others groaned in barbershop-quartet harmony, as if this had all been rehearsed many times. Perhaps it had. Maybe he had come this way before. The driver gagged, drew away, and rolled his eyes again, this time going in the other direction.

Somebody was dead.

Cal jumped off the bus in one off-balanced leap and ran splashing across the Avenue through the slush, heading toward his dorm. Blood spattered everywhere. He didn't hear the blaring horns and nearly got flattened by a speeding Mustang, the driver skidding almost into the curb before gaining control and wheeling off. Cal stared on and the guy gave him the finger.

No real thoughts yet, only a blind state of motion. He was going too slow and the frustration started to crack his chest apart. His sister floated alongside him, her robes flowing wildly and snapping in the wind. She was saying something, she was always saying something, but he never wanted to hear it. He wanted to cover his ears, but there were giant gashes in his hands. He sprinted for his room because somewhere inside himself he stupidly believed that the spilling of blood would have to take place there, as upon any sacred sacrificial altar. As if someone could not die elsewhere.

"Jodi," he whispered.

Night glistened with moonlight gliding off the embankments of snow. The darkness pooled and eddied and swam from spot to spot. He slid on a patch of ice in front of one of the frat houses, dropped to all fours and skidded on his shins into a load of trash heavy with empty pizza boxes and a million beer cans. The crackling bones in his knees were exceptionally loud.

Sharp twinges skewered his calves. He cried out as he came to a crumpled stop against the dumpster. A curtain drew back on the second floor and a thick pair of glasses peered down at him.

Someone's dead.

When Cal regained his footing the acrid stench caught him full thrust in the nostrils. He turned, and his sister wove before him, trying to catch his eye. The whiskey, it was the whiskey. He held up his hand as if to ward her off, but he could still see her face through the holes in his palms. Wind pummeled him back into the trash, streaming upward from under his fists so that the stink of blood lifted high and blew into his face like a shotgun blast. Above, the thick glasses fogged the windowpane and let the curtains fall back into place.

Caleb hit the quad and immediately doubled over, trying to staunch the flow of blood with the wads of his torn pocket lining. The bleeding wouldn't stop no matter what he did. The crimson splashes ran down his coat. Balled bits of cotton were too small to fill the spike holes in his hands. They absorbed blood and became squishy, then shredded and dropped through the gashes to the ground. Cal ran awkwardly. His legs threatened to slip out from under him the same way he'd flounced into the dean and his wife. Snowfall had thinned—or had it thickened?—into driving hail. He could see better than before, though, and now everyone could see him as well. This was going to get even uglier.

Coming from their night classes, the other students swelled around him: standing in doorways chatting about assignments, bustling past heading for dinner, running for shelter across the lawns as the freezing rain came beating down. He looked for a friendly face, searching for Jodi.

Those who noticed him stopped in their tracks. His math professor gave a bleat of animal terror. A jock carrying a laughing girl over his shoulder fireman style veered wildly. Her husky giggling ended as if chopped by an ax. "Hee hee hee, holy shit . . . !" Her boyfriend spun, kicking up snow, and when his eyes focused on Caleb the guy nearly dumped her on her head.

Running made the blood spill faster. He had no idea just how much he could afford to lose before he'd pass out. There was absolutely no pain. There'd never been any discomfort the other times he'd suffered the stigmata, only a hideous confusion. He held up his palms before his eyes, watching the dark, murky nail holes closing too slowly . . . or were they closing at all? He couldn't really tell in the shadows. Perhaps his sister would know, if only he had the courage to ask her. A group of kids shouted meaninglessly at him.

He knew it looked as though he'd murdered somebody: cut a throat, stabbed ten people through the heart. Is this what the guy had looked like after killing Sylvia Campbell?

Cal snarled—some of the ghosts that had tortured his sister now tormented him in turn. This must be the way it worked. The lessons being passed on, one to the other. He checked around to see if a green van was coming for him. Memories not even yours could still haunt you to death.

The failed nun had managed to perform a miracle after all. She'd been bathed up to the elbows in blood at least once a week working the street: watching the rats take out chunks of infants, the homeless set on fire and pissed on, the suicides who hadn't quite made it, and those who had. He tried to press her back into her grave, but she wouldn't go. This was resurrection. And now where was she leading him?

"Jesus, God. Jodi." He tightened his fists, and his curled middle fingers poked into his palms and up through the back of his hands.

Freezing rain pelted at him as if he were being stoned, ice crystals bouncing off his neck, slithering down his collar.

Professor Yokver came out of his office in Camden Hall, with his klackity-klak puppet arms flailing and his hefty briefcase—assuredly filled with failures—clasped tightly in one hand. Chalk dust still clung to him, adding an extra nimbus to him in the eerie light. The long ponytail popped out from beneath a heavy wool hat. With his eyes wide he caught sight of Caleb and made an appalled yet extremely pleased face. There was an incredible depth beneath that goddamn silly mask.

"Fuck you, Yok," Cal said, and kept running.

Blood spattered the snow, speckling the white.

Someone's dead.

He finally got to his dorm, legs throbbing and weak and feeling horribly twisted, but no worse off than the inside of his own head. His sister's habit kept blocking his view. Even through the explosion of noise he'd made rushing into the building, slamming the heavy door behind him and huffing for breath, bleeding all over the place, the girl sitting at the security desk didn't look up. She was reading Stephen King's *Bag of Bones* and listening to Bauhaus's "Bela Lugosi's Dead" on her Walkman so loudly that the music spilled from her headphones. Cal wanted to scream, but she only would have ignored him.

He skirted the empty lounge and took off toward his room, fumbling for the key, hands and coat now sticky with his drying blood. His scalp tightened as sweat trickled down his sideburns and hail melted in his hair. Bloody palm prints were all over the place.

The keys fell through his hand. A wave of dizziness shook him, and he held his breath to keep from vomiting.

As he bent to retrieve them, leaning against the knob, the door opened.

He viciously shook his head once, dazed and unsure if he'd locked his room before leaving for the library this morning. He recalled the possibility that the door had been open earlier when he'd rushed to answer the phone. Cal gritted his teeth, almost hoping for knives, just so long as there was something he could touch.

Entering, Caleb half expected Jo to be waiting for him, lying on the bed. Either ready to massage the knots from his shoulders or coming on strong for Rose, or maybe pouting about the winter carnival, or gutted in the corner, sprayed back against the already stained wall.

Once inside he realized his mistake in returning to his own room instead of heading directly to Jodi's.

His instincts for death had brought him home instead.

"Oh, you fucking idiot, you stupidass fucking shithead," he hissed, unaware that he'd spoken, even while he listened.

He threw his coat in the closet, grabbed a clean pair of socks out of his drawer, and wrapped them snugly around his hands, then picked the telephone off the floor where he'd left it after getting the dead air crank this morning. The receiver was cracked, but the dial tone wailed aimlessly. He called Jo's room, but there was no answer. After eight anguish-building rings he threw the phone against the wall again, and watched it splinter and ricochet.

It was getting late.

Much too late. Baby noises of anguish filled his throat. He checked his blood-smeared watch and saw it was almost eight o'clock. Jo might've just gone over to the dean's party without him, or perhaps she and Rose had decided to swear off men entirely and were out there somewhere together.

Or, Christ, one or the other might be as dead as his sister and parents, as Sylvia Campbell or Circe or whoever she was, or maybe someone else lay eviscerated nearby. Bodies might be hidden all over campus, undiscovered. Under his floorboards, buried outside the front door.

He looked in the closet again, pushing aside his clothes. He opened the window and stuck out his head, gasping. He wanted to shriek, and he didn't want to shriek.

These socks knotted around his hands hadn't soaked up too much blood. He slowly untied them. The bleeding had stopped. Considering the size of the wounds, he again wondered why there wasn't any pain or nerve damage. The holes had shrunk to the size of quarters. He tossed the socks in the closet too.

He had to find Jo.

A hammering at the door startled him backward into the bedpost. Somebody wanted in badly. He saw film-clip scenarios flicker past: Rose with her sharpened nails wanting to skin him inch by inch; Fruggy Fred snapping awake long enough to talk about the perchances to dream; the dean finally feeling hunger, on his knees and begging for a morsel of food.

Once again the door hadn't been properly closed. The latch rested tightly against the jamb but hadn't completely locked shut. With a soft creaking the door swung open, haunted house style, boogie man creeping in the hall. The sudden draft caught two small squares of blue paper lying on the floor, and they fluttered across the room—a note he'd missed in his mad scramble to get inside. It had to be from Jodi. Christ, please.

Bull Winkle stood there in the doorway with sleet dripping off his Brillo pad eyebrows and his security guard slicker. His thinning gray hair stood in scraggly tufts that pointed to New Mexico, Australia, the Tundra. Veins bulged in the corners of Bull's black troubled eyes, and his squat muscular frame seemed ready to launch at the word *go*. Caleb had no doubt Bull could clear the distance in one shot. He had always known a a meeting of some kind was bound to take place between them. Since the first day of the term, a drastic change had occurred in at least one of their personalities; shapes bend. Nothing felt stable or amiable anymore.

The radiator rattled on. The top page of the note curled and crept another inch closer. Cal kept his fists at his sides, hoping nothing could be seen in the dim light. It wouldn't work, of course; he'd left a trail all across campus leading right back here. He tensed his abdominal muscles because they always went for the stomach first. Bull's callused hand appeared to be the size of a forge, and Cal wished very badly that Bull wouldn't beat him up.

"What in the hell happened to you?" Bull said, staring wide-eyed. "What have you done?"

"I haven't done anything." Caleb's ability to lie astounded him at times, and his frustration vanished beneath a carefully controlled plastic armor exterior. You could do it sometimes, when you needed to. He knew he had no choice—that he very seldom had any choice at all. Someone was dead, and his hands were covered with blood.

"Are you cut? Did you cut somebody?" Bull asked.

"A dog got hit on the Avenue."

"All of this, from a dog?"

"I wanted to help, but there was nothing that could be done. I tried making it comfortable, but the poor mutt died in the snow. The driver didn't stop."

"Up on the Avenue." Bull nodded and stood a little straighter, the hands poised and ready. It was like watching a Cro-Magnon man rising to become Neanderthal. "What kind?"

"A Buick."

"What kind of dog?"

Cal gave a one-shouldered shrug. He noticed Bull's nostrils as he sniffed the air—good, good, did he smell it too? Even beneath all the new blood, the scent of another murder? It might be worth it, getting rapped on the jaw, just so long as somebody else felt Circe in the room. "Like I

171

said, it was a mutt, and mangled. What difference does it make?"

"None."

"Retriever, I think. A golden retriever, maybe with some lab in it."

"Professor Yokver called security—"

Oh Yok, you sissy bastard.

"—saying that you were shouting foul language over the square and running around like a madman, something like that. Sprinting across campus with blood covering your hands."

"He was right, more or less."

"So I see. I know the professor has a particularly bad habit of overemphasizing just about everything where his students are concerned, but I guess this time he called it on the mark. Why were you cursing him?"

"Because he's a prick and I don't like him."

There was nearly a grin in Bull's eyes, though his face darkened. "Well, I do believe that's a good reason."

Cal caught the older man's steady gaze and kept hold without wavering. "I'm late for the dean's party and I don't want to piss him off. My girlfriend has already left without me."

His hands, Jesus, were the holes closing? What could be seen?

"Oh, yeah?" Bull said, scratching his stubbled

throat. "What, you're invited to that shindig?"

"Yes."

"Must've been one hell of a smashed-up animal to make such a mess out of you that way, getting blood all over the walls, everyplace. I could follow the spotted trail right through the snow part of the way."

"I wanted to help it."

"Yeah, nothing deserves to die hurting and alone."

One beat, and then another. "No, no one does."

The bells rang eight times.

Neither one caught the full gist of what was happening here, Caleb thought, as Bull drew back his chin and inspected the room, understanding that more than once something had occurred here involving gore. He took in the busted phone, the shards of glass on the floor from the busted peanut butter jar, the rest of the mess.

Where were the cops anyway? . . . why hadn't they stopped by to question him yet? Three fucking weeks. Did Bull know her files had all been lies, and did anyone care? Did he read the "Jacked-In" column, or did everybody miss it? Were there other considerations to take into account?

"What's going on?" Cal murmured. It was an

all-inclusive question; let Bull take it any way he wanted to. Caleb felt as wired as Rose had been, with just as many unnatural colors in his face. Was Sylvia Campbell simply a computer glitch? Had it all been a mistake? He tried to act as casual as he could, glancing down to inspect the damage. His hands had completely healed. His middle fingers caressed the sealed flesh of his sweaty palms.

"What, I have to tell you?" Bull said.

"Huh?"

"What's going on." They were working at cross-purposes, or perhaps they had the same purpose but just couldn't talk about it. "You're the one who's supposed to be telling me."

"I wish I could."

"How do you sleep in here?"

"How would you, Bull?"

He put some thought into it. "I think if I was the kind of guy who stopped to help dying dogs in the snow, I would've gotten myself transferred to another room. I would've gotten the hell out of here, probably. I think most everybody would have left, even moved to a whole other dorm."

"Following that line of reasoning," Cal said, "then I should move to another college altogether, and everyone should leave the university with me. Except—"

Bull picked up on it. "Following that line of reasoning means you'd have no place to go, not anywhere. Not even home. Maybe especially not there."

Now, hey, hey, wasn't *that* the goddamn truth.

"Did they find him?" Cal asked.

"Why didn't you wash your hands?"

"The man who murdered the girl who called herself Sylvia Campbell, in my room, Bull. Did they find him? Have you stopped him?"

"No." And after another lengthy silence. "Have you?"

"No."

They stared at each other.

"You might want to put that girl on probation," Cal said, sounding strangely gentle, even to himself.

"What, the one reading at the security desk going deaf from the music? I already mean to."

"Where's Rocky?"

The question seemed to annoy him. "I don't know." He fumbled with his belt. "If you see him, tell him I was looking for him." Bull's voice and gaze drifted, and he swayed on the balls of his feet. "I'll let you get on to that big soiree. I wouldn't want you to miss out on the fine conversation, all that shrimp in cocktail sauce. Don't curse out anybody else; the dean might not take kindly to it." Bull closed the door behind him, and it resounded shut with a loud clack.

Caleb couldn't shake the idea that a compromise—perhaps a partnership—had just been made.

He bent and grabbed the two-page note off the floor and read Jodi's graceful script:

It took me a while, but I was finally able to calm Rose down. For what it's worth, I believe you. I know you weren't lying to her, but you could have handled the situation with more sensitivity. I can't help feeling that you've let her down, as well as yourself, in the process. You're probably on a binge somewhere. Get home safely. I'll be at the dean's party. Rose is coming with me. The dean invited a number of select members of the senior class. I don't know why Fruggy was invited, except perhaps as a joke. Tell Willy not to show up, if he has any compassion for her at all. You probably simply lost your invitation, Cal. You've lost a great deal of yourself this year.

Christ, give a guy a fucking break.

Please don't come by tonight. I know you'll make a scene. It's not entirely your fault,

but you will, especially if you've had anything to drink, which I know you have. Get
some sleep, and we'll talk it all through in
the morning. Sleep in my bed—my friend
Sheila is on desk until one in the morning
and she'll let you in. I'll be back early. I wish
you weren't forever so far away.

Cal went to the bathroom and took a long
scalding shower, standing under the steaming
jets until the last vestiges of the alcoholic daze
were gone. He scrubbed at the blood; it washed
off more easily than he'd thought. Shades of
Macbeth returned. His blood swirled down the
drain, looking less real than the chocolate syrup
Hitchcock used in *Psycho*.

He shaved, then dressed in the only black suit
he owned, wearing a white shirt and black tie,
a pair of cuff links and a tiepin that had be-
longed to his father. Lady Dean's "nothing too
extravagant" was only a ruse, of course—their
social affairs were never informal. The dean
and his wife put the funk in perfunctory. In the
middle of a blizzard she'd worn a mink. They
would all look their best.

He checked himself in the mirror, straightening his tie, then put on his black London Fog
overcoat.

He wished there was more of his father in

him. His dad had been a gentle and honest man, blue collar, with forearms like Popeye, who didn't give much of a damn for higher education.

The power of symbolism was never lost on Cal. He noticed just how much he looked like he was going to a funeral.

Someone was dead.

And she would be at the party.

Chapter Ten

For all of this, the night grew uncommonly still.

Skies had cleared, and the chill wind became so crisp it almost felt like heat. Snow cleaved to the tops of trees that dipped and swayed like the hydrocephalic kids trying to play tag in the fields.

But quietly. Silver threads of light lit the thick ice on branches; myriads of sparkles and rainbows shimmered in darkness. Breath curled like kittens. Tormented shadows crawled against the surging snowdrifts down the path. These woods pulled all the right triggers of his fixation.

He knew the place well.

Lady Dean and the dean lived about a mile

from the northern edge of campus, back through the thickets found directly behind Jodi's dorm. Instead of going up and around to the Avenue, he took the shortcut, trudging through the snow. Over the years, the wild groves bordering the football field had thickened to make a small forest, a romantic spot if you were inclined to think along those lines.

Last spring, every afternoon for a couple of weeks, he and Jo had picnicked and made love beneath the green rooftop thatches. There they'd familiarized themselves with one another's tender areas, memorizing the curves and hard lines of each other's bodies. That was right after he'd read Thoreau's *Walden* and been caught up on this back-to-nature kick, as he and Jo wrestled on the carpets of matted flowers and leaves, and the birds looked down at them mysteriously and the squirrels went crazy and chittered in alarm.

There was an ephemeral sense of earth magic here, so fleeting he couldn't be sure if he actually felt it. His sister wafted along, rushing through the brush ahead of him, as if keeping watch. She kept trying to get his attention and he kept looking away.

This was also the perfect setting for a knife kill splatter movie: where the bodies were laid out half-exposed in shallow graves, and they came tumbling out of the branches. You had a girl running through the brush with one of her tits hanging out, wearing cutoff shorts even in winter, staring back over her shoulder as she jiggled and worked her lungs, and came barreling right into the killer's outthrust hand holding the machete. She'd do the same thing in the next movie, too, and in the one after that, except her tits would be even bigger then. For a minute you'd wonder why she never learned, and then you'd remember that she was getting paid.

Snow spiraled across the copses, and naked elms swung over to clap Caleb's back as he passed by. He nearly let out a shout. Fresh dog tracks littered the area as though the ghost of a rundown retriever mutt had risen from his lie, to meet with him on common ground. He hoped someone would soon clean his blood off the walls.

The winter carnival had been set up on the fields at the opposite edge of the forest. A sea of moonlight surged and rippled, and he saw reflections off the tops of rides. He'd ridden the whirligig and cup and saucer with his sister, the carousel and merry-go-round. He'd laughed wildly as she sat across from him smiling sadly. She must've seen rats covering everybody all the time.

The movie of his own imagination rolled on

and on, backward and forward, hearing the slice of a kitchen knife into cantaloupe, the girl gurgling up red syrup, the audience munching popcorn, make-out moans in the back row, and the director yelling cut.

He also heard muted music and laughter.

The nun nodded and pointed. Shaking slush from his shoes, Cal wandered out of the grove onto the dean's property. He walked around the side of the piazza, past a double set of frosted glass doors, skirting the wide U-shaped drive-way and the vast front yard beyond. The large house stood out beautifully in this polar milieu: a combination high-rise ranch and Miami designer beachfront architecture, all glass, wood, brick, and open space. It looked as if it had walked all over hell and then finally hunkered down, nestling in the dirt.

Costly cars lined the entire length of the street; he spotted a couple of Jags, Corvettes, Porsches, and a handful of other sports cars, and the mayor's limo. Informal, all right, but of course. The valet parking attendants looked at him uneasily, holding onto their Thermoses, as he moved out from the darkness.

Scanning the rest of the block, Cal registered that the nearest neighbors were a hundred yards off to each side of the dean's property, tucked away behind walls of neatly trimmed evergreens. Professor Yokver lived down the street maybe a quarter of a mile, where the neighborhood changed over to mediocrity.

Cal had been to the dean's house only twice before, once invited for lunch with other students back during orientation, and again last year, when he'd been asked by Lady Dean to drop off Anne Sexton's *42 Mercy Street*, a book of poetry Cal had held overdue from the library for a month. They'd had an intelligent yet passionless discussion on suicide-poets and shared a glass of iced tea. He couldn't quite remember whether he'd had a good time.

He sidled up to the windows and saw the blinding chandelier and ostentatious candelabras burning in various rooms.

Most of his professors were there, chatting animatedly inside. Howard Moored, head of the English department, his fluffy white beard and shock of gray hair swaying as he intensely acted out some involved joke, with the others listening politely, hinging on the punch line so they could get out of the circle.

Over there, Denise Bernstein, his drama professor, with her short doughy fingers stuffing a piece of lime into a bottle of Corona beer, accidentally spritzing Howard so that he reeled backward into a caterer walking by with a tray of hors d'oeuvres. If you watched them all together, it was sort of like a sitcom.

Iggy Geotz, sociology professor and Cal's project adviser, reaching for Howard and catching him solidly, perfectly, holding him the way teachers held their power over grades. All the rest of them laughing and mingling, drinking, relaxing, and uptight with the notion of tenure held out like carrots. Yokver wasn't to be seen. Where the hell was he?

Students he knew from past classes were talking amiably while others wandered without purpose, puzzled by the circus atmosphere, seeing their teachers so drawn out of familiar character. Cal couldn't call even one of them his friend. Still more faces he only vaguely recognized drifted past, and he was unsure of where he might have seen them before. Elderly alumni, town officials, and more unknown names from the college board moved in and out of view. Cal was dressed a lot better than most of them. He felt an odd pride that others had fallen for Lady Dean's deceit and he hadn't.

KLAP hummed softly over the stereo. Cal walked around and shoved at the front door. He was almost swept backward when the suffocating wave of body heat inside swelled forward against him. He checked his hands and hoped there was no lingering blood scent on him.

The Night Class

Cal eyed the crowd and they eyed him back. Shishka Bob's voice introduced another Zenith Brite song. It meant Bob was in a bad mood. "Time for the queen of the evening to cuddle up to us again, yeah, as she plays the harp of your heart, plucking at your soul, just the way you like it at the moment." At least Bob got that much right. "Even clawing at your back, if you're really lucky. But you aren't, now are you, you poor bitches and bastards?"

Don't call me up, baby, unless you want the
    whole truth
about the difference between the living and
    the dead
You've got honor and horror, but you just
    don't know
which end is which
and you whine when you want to be fed
but you don't have the couth
of youth, oh no
not anymore

Caleb stood in the main hallway. From his position he witnessed the moon framed in the bay windows, smears of flickering candle flame glowing against the glass. His sister's reflection flitted across the panes, her hair disheveled, mouth open to speak. Two or three of his class-

185

mates turned and called his name, and he absently waved but didn't move toward them.

"Have you seen Jodi?" Cal asked, and was mostly ignored. Some folks shook their heads.

One of the economics professors stumbled into him, and Cal could smell the rum on the man, fused to halitosis. Without warning the nausea rose in his belly again—rum would always do it to him from now on. He wondered if his tenacity would ever allow him to forget the incisions of his failures, or if he would forever repeat the process, trapped as Sylvia Campbell was in her own sketch. The economics professor laughed maniacally at nothing visible and reeled away.

Julia Blanders, his creative writing professor, scooted from what must have been an unbearably boring corner of the room, breaking free from several men without a word. She rushed to him with her drink raised high, eyebrows knitted in a way that urged him to come to her rescue. Caleb tried to smile, but his lips wouldn't do what they were supposed to. He flapped his London Fog open in a gesture of helplessness, and she came forward and reached behind his back to hug him with an intolerably light touch. It struck him as such a motherly gesture that he suddenly wanted to fall into her arms and start sobbing like a baby.

"Have you seen Jodi?" he asked.

"No," she said. "Oh wait, maybe. A while ago. I can't remember. It's now an established fact: Dullness kills brain cells. Everyone eventually merges at these damn functions, until we're all one immense piece of pulled taffy."

"You didn't know that until tonight?"

"Let's say I had my suspicions." She bit into the lemon peel in her drink and let the rind cover her teeth. He saw that she had a bruise on her chin, hidden by some pancake, but the makeup had smeared with her sweat. He wondered if she'd been stumbling drunk and had done it to herself. She sucked out the pulp and swallowed. "I didn't think you'd be invited to this one, Cal."

"I wasn't really," he said, the ire rising, slipping so easily back into place. "Why'd you think that?"

"Because it's a party full of ass-kissers."

"Not you."

"Oh, yes, me. Me, big time. You don't think I'm really any different from the rest of them, do you?"

"Let's say I had my suspicions."

He stared, knowing she wasn't really much older than he was—late twenties, maybe thirty, with darkly rich red hair, pale good looks, and caramel freckles that should have married her off to a cardiac specialist. Yet she was as inextricably bound to the university as he was.

Julia couldn't keep the distaste out of her voice. "I wouldn't want to seem anything less than warmhearted and amicable, now would I? Perhaps ingratiating is the proper word placed in the suitable context." She was big on proper words, always marking up his papers and writing *awkward* whenever he went overboard with metaphor. He did it a lot.

"Academia has its pitfalls," he said. It sounded deep but stupid at the same time, which put it into suitable context.

"We do what we must for the sake of appearances. I'm still looking for tenure. Observe how Iggy and Howard are trying so desperately to be both witty and appealing. And they've had tenure for twenty years. You're never out of the game."

Imagine going the long haul and having to be charming until you retired, always smiling as if your dentures didn't fit. "I didn't think they had it in them."

"No, not many do, but they're troupers. They can degrade themselves with the best of them."

"I never thought of it that way."

"No, you wouldn't," Julia said with the smooth lilt of an insult, and finished off her drink in one long slurp. "You're too ethical, Cal. We've heard about you."

It struck him hard, especially the word *ethical*. Yok was talking to people. "What does that mean, Julia?"

"Not a damn thing, really."

The mayor glided over and whispered in her ear, and Julia let out a guffaw that made Cal wince, as she made an awful effort to bat her eyes. She didn't have the knack to be a flirt, but she went through the motions anyway. Every incisor showed in an effervescent smile, the laugh hideously loud, bellowing from down in her diaphragm, where it probably hurt.

Her hand was perfectly placed on the mayor's chest, fingers plying in small circles, now back and forth, nails lightly scratching like she was about to go kitchy-coo. It reminded him of Candida Celeste wrangling for cash. Another bellow and the mayor giggled like a teenage girl and went skipping back to his wife. Cal guessed it didn't matter how well you played the game, so long as it worked.

Yeeaah
Don't cuddle up to me
Don't you cuddle up to me
Don't you dare crawl to me, don't you call to
    me

189

Noooo
Don't cuddle up to me
Don't you cuddle up to me

"Patrons of the arts," Julia said, tearing two fresh drinks from a waiter with a wasted face, the emptiness of cancer in it. "One and all. A lot of green is switching hands tonight, an abundance of gifts given out to us, who are legion. If you get on the train maybe one day we'll name a hall after you."

"Undoubtedly," Cal said. He'd respected all her red-penned comments on paper, but now—still trying to bat her eyes like Hedy Lamarr, but her lashes were too thin—he couldn't see the teacher in her anymore. She appeared as lost and filled with loathing as he usually did. "Why invite the students?"

"They're the biggest ass-kissers of all. They keep the rest of us spry and content and empowered." Lit by the candelabras, her red hair appeared ignited by the flames, ashen face tinged by the glow. "Why else do you think I keep you around, Cal? Just because of your good looks?"

"I think you've had too much tonight, Julia."

"Too much what? Liquor? Not even nearly enough, trust me. Here." She handed him her own half-filled glass and he slammed it back, hating the taste of gin but not caring much. "You must have been more thirsty than you thought. Come, I'll make us another."

"No. I'm not liking you much tonight."

"You'll like me better later on tonight," she told him, and put her hand to his chest, fingers again moving in small circles, now back and forth, as if in a finely detailed performance, nails lightly scratching, and now harder, deeper, as he felt his skin about to break.

"No, I don't think I will," he said. "Go play with the mayor. I'm quitting. I'm leaving school tonight." The flatness of his statement caught him as flush as it did her. Until he'd actually said it, he hadn't known how much he hated this place, but the instant it was out he realized he'd always wanted to go, and would have to go now.

"No! Listen to me, you don't want to do that! It would be a dreadful mistake. Cal . . . !"

"Get away from me."

His actions seemed jerky in the fullest measure of the word. Like a tangled marionette being yanked along a backyard stage, and also like a total jerk. He knew he was changing too slowly. He could not squander what little courage he had managed to gather. Movement skimmed across his peripheral vision, and he kept turning, then turning again.

He searched for Jodi, and Willy and Rose and Fruggy Fred, but he didn't see any of them in the parlor, the dining room, or the alcoves. Howard Moored said hello and gave Caleb's arm a paternal squeeze. The din drowned out Shishka Bob, and Cal felt as though he'd lost another friend.

Iggy Geotz swung over as Cal passed the bar. Iggy hugged him wildly and said, "Another?"

"Excuse me?"

"What's that on your breath? Scotch? Gin? On the rocks?"

Jesus, God, he never knew so many of them could put this much liquor away. Cal wanted a shot desperately. He swallowed hard. The university made them all etherize themselves. "No."

Iggy shrugged and banged bottles and ice buckets so that they chimed rude melodies. He won a quick tug-of-war with a short priest when they both went for the same bottle. Iggy swore, returned, and said, "Pip-squeak bastard tried to shut me out. I thought they only drank wine, goddamn highbrow Jesuits."

"But—"

"Teaches a night class in socio-theology, always trying to steal my student base away." The priest kept throwing him nasty looks. Iggy spun to shake a fist, and Cal made a play for an open corner of the room. Iggy stopped him, though, sticking out his arm on a level with Cal's throat, like he was trying to clothesline him. "You haven't shown me your projected thesis. I've been meaning to ask you about it. How's the work coming along?"

"It's killing me," he said, putting the emphasis in the right place, and hoped his chuckle cut it. "Have you seen Jodi?"

"Who?"

"Jodi, my lady." Iggy knew damn well who Jo was. Why was everyone pretending they had no idea who she was? "My girlfriend."

"Oh, yes, the blonde who used to wait outside class for you? No, I haven't seen her tonight. For some reason I was under the impression the two of you were no longer an item."

"Of course we're still together."

"My mistake."

What did his professors pick up on that he was missing? She was all right; she had to be all right. For the first time he smiled, dry lips catching on his teeth, forming an inert grin. "You're another fucking prick, Iggy."

He spun away and looked at a multimirrored wall, edged in white marble and surrounded by the repeated ad infinitum flames of candles. Motion in the glass caught his eye, and at the middle of it was a daub of whirling black.

A shade waiting for him as if summoned by his grin.

Fruggy Fred's whispered words resounded clearly.

Caleb stared at the ghost of Sylvia Campbell. *Circe.*

Except it wasn't. He blinked and refocused, which took everything he had, and saw Lady Dean standing at the top of the staircase behind him.

Their gazes met in the mirror, and he forced himself to raise his chin so he didn't look whipped already. She crooked her finger, beckoning him to follow.

Her lips were set, showing him the way. Oh boy. Lady Dean drifted down the stairs, threading through the crowd with all the litheness of a ballerina, not letting anybody touch her. He moved. Julia Blanders approached him again, then noticed the lady's trajectory. "Whew," she breathed, "maybe I was wrong about you, Cal. Maybe you'll make it after all."

"How about if I just give you a boot in your ass?"

She laughed and wafted from him as if dust.

Lady Dean stood drop-dead gorgeous, decked in a tight-fitting black dressing gown with a dazzling diamond choker, mouth as crimson as the bathroom tiles. Conversations stopped dead as men in the vicinity went numb in her presence; you could hear the starched collars creaking as heads turned.

Her hair had been brushed in a high-arcing sweep that tumbled over one side of her face, a style similar to that worn by Sylvia Campbell in the sketch folded inside his wallet, and inside his skull. It would be extremely bad to get those two confused in his mind at this late point of his obsession.

"Cal, I'm so pleased you could make it," Lady Dean said in that toneless voice. He wasn't certain if he should call her Clarissa. He knew that would be overstepping his bounds—especially now that he was going to leave. Her face, for all its beauty, was merely a delicate mask of flesh held in place by a tight array of muscle. It looked ready to drop at any second. He could imagine her features on the floor, broken like dashed porcelain.

"Thanks for having me," he told her.

"My, you're dressed ravishingly. I don't believe I've ever had the pleasure of seeing you in a suit before. Let me stare at those healthy red cheeks for a moment. You look positively . . . cherubic."

He had never been called cherubic before, and he didn't like it. He tried to keep the growl out of his throat but didn't do too good a job. "Thank you. Have you seen Jodi?"

"Your lovely girlfriend is in the parlor, chatting with my husband about the latest developments in medicinal psychotherapy." *Thank Christ she's all right!* "Or so they were only a few minutes ago." So now the lady had no problem remembering who Jodi was. She touched his wrist without the delicacy that most people inclined to touch wrists in conversation will offer. "Though I wasn't at all sure if you would be in attendance tonight."

"I apologize for being late."

"Oh, don't be silly." She pulled the empty glass out of his hand, which he hadn't realized he'd been holding. "It appears you need another drink. Please allow me to make you one."

"No, thank you. I've had enough." He saw the other men watching him, avoiding eye contact, either jealous or simply wishing him luck. He wondered how many had been in this position before, and who had survived and how they did it. Maybe none of them.

"You seem to be at a loss for words tonight, Cal."

"No," he answered, struggling to come up with something but already having lost the words.

She reveled in his discomfort, but he didn't

blame her much. It was the sort of weakness you looked for in other people. He figured he would have gotten a kick out of it too, if only there had ever been a time he held such authority. Perhaps she waited for him to compliment her, but in a weird fashion he knew it would only make him look foolish, making frail comments like the rest of them. He continued to scan for Jodi, but he could really only see Lady Dean.

"Would you like to dance?" she asked. "Regardless of the fact that I'll be known as a philistine, I've already changed the radio station to something a bit more classical. I enjoy it so."

"Dance?"

See, there it was again. He couldn't finish a sentence.

"Yes. Dance. Whereby we sway about to music, standing close together with arms about one another, preferably. Dance."

It stopped him. "Wait a minute."

"Yes?"

"You just made a joke?"

She nodded, and rivers of veins in her neck pulsed beneath the diamond choker. "Cal, let me ask you. Are you aware that you've never directly addressed me by any appellation?"

Now there was a proper word. "Appell—"

"That you've never once said, 'Mrs.' Or

Tom Piccirilli

'ma'am' or even 'Clarissa' or anything at all?"

He knew it, all right. "I'm sorry." Again with an apology. He half-expected her to come back and hit him with one of the Yok's *Pshaw, young master, don't be sorry.* He wasn't, he truly wasn't, so why did he keep saying he was?

"Don't be. I find it mildly refreshing."

"Why is that?" He didn't fall for it and say her name. There was no reason to change tonight.

"I don't know. I just do. Please dance with me."

"All right," he assented, and wondered how much he was empowering her in doing so.

She led him out of the dining area. They wandered past the pip-squeak priest, who stared at her with a feral glare that would cost him big time in the confessional. Lady Dean paced Cal down through another hall, moving under the starlit skylights toward the back of the house. They kept going and going, receding farther into her realm. He followed like a puppy.

They passed the double set of glass doors and a large antique breakfront filled with Dresden figurines. The house appeared to be rippling now, the shadows crawling like fog around his feet. They came to those type of iron gates that close off corridors for no reason, black railings that fit in with the Spanish decor and velvet matadors that everyone found so delightful in the '70s. Whoever had decorated this place didn't know exactly where or when he lived.

Cal slipped on spilled wine and skidded to a stop on the tile. Lady Dean twisted into him. She smiled a genuine smile this time, carnivorous in its duplicity. It scared the shit out of him.

She shut the gates behind them. His breath seeped from him.

"Dance with me," she implored.

Teach me. Forgive me.

"Where?"

"Here."

"But there's no music."

"Yes, there is."

She stepped forward and kissed his neck, her arms locked down and tense at her sides, which surprised him, with her nails hooking on the hem of her gown. She breathed into him, lifting her skirt now over her knees, raising it still higher as he witnessed the slow spread of thigh. He watched with such intensity that his vision grew bright along the edges. The widening extent of flesh was too much like a growing pool of blood. Caleb stepped away and got hung up in his overcoat. She pushed. He fell back heavily against a door. She shoved her face into his throat and sucked and licked.

"Let's go to bed. Dance with me there."

"Ah, hey now, listen—"

She held his shoulders against the door and slid her heavy breasts across his chest. His father's tiepin angled to one side as her tongue started swabbing him somewhere near his Adam's apple, and she didn't stop until she'd licked up to his earlobe. Then she did it again, and again, and once more. He had balled his fists and kept looking at her body, thinking of where he should hit her. Everything was wrong. Or maybe everything just wasn't wrong enough.

"Say my name," she told him.

He couldn't give in. Names held power. "No."

"Say it."

"No."

"Clarissa. Do it." She laughed, but there was nothing alive in there. "Do it, Caleb."

The blushing fire in his face embarrassed him even more, as his hard-on strained and he began to sneer at himself. So much of him wanted to go out with this bang. Her breathing slowed and grew harsher. Her movements became snakelike and explosive as her writhing curves bucked against him in all the proper places. Clarissa undid his tie and yanked the first two buttons off his shirt, biting his chest hair. Cal tried to back up—maybe to get away or maybe just to get better positioning—but he was already up against the doorknob. His arms were plastered out against the frame as though he were stuck on a whirligig with his sister again.

"Dance," Lady Dean purred.

"Don't," he whispered, without strength, without the slightest resolve to do anything he could put a name to. He still wanted to slug her; perhaps that was a good sign, perhaps not. How, exactly, had it come to this? He looked at the new flesh of his palms and wondered if he had the willpower to slap her, or whether he'd immediately begin to bleed once more. She moved closer, her hips on top of his, as he clumsily took her in his arms and pressed his mouth over hers, trying to consume her in one swallow and then be done with it.

She teased and pecked. "Yes."

"Why?" he asked. "Why?" And then he couldn't say even that.

She laced fingers with him and motioned for him to grab her breasts. He lifted his hands and looked at them again, knowing somebody was dead and not caring so much right now. He didn't want the sex but got off on the affirmation, the validation that he existed, even here in this awful place. She brushed her thighs against his wrists and touched the doorknob.

It turned and he scrambled backward, falling through the open doorway. Laughing loudly with little yipping barks of malignancy, she

201

dropped on top of him and drove him down hard. They hit in a tangle on the bedroom carpet. He stared up at her as she straddled him. The lady moaned.

Caleb groaned, and so did Circe.

Someone else moaned.

It was a painfully familiar sound, so well known that it took a second to place. He spun and looked at the bed.

You can die.

You can die and come back in the same second, and just not want to be alive anymore.

"Oh my Christ," he whimpered.

"We're just in time," Clarissa told him.

In time to see Jodi lying naked with silver strands of saliva draping her tits, a swell of red rising on her belly, two small scratches at her neck. A look of intense pleasure redefined her face, filling it with bliss, her tongue lolling farther than it ought to be able, unleashed with mad gratification.

Jo's body heaved as if giving birth, a cadaver looming above her: bones came grating together above her, fingers like spiders working at his woman, a mouth veering, twisting, and curling into a crazed smile that just kept going on and on and on, with so many teeth they didn't seem to start or stop in the jaw.

Bodies bucked and slammed together, both

of them grinding in perfectly timed thrusts that proved this had happened many times before. Her blond hair everywhere, layered like a wreath set down at the feet of her love, as the dead struggled to please the living, feeding on eternal misery, that skeleton grinning in rictus, turning now to stare straight into the dying eyes of Caleb Prentiss.

Everything became very red.

Chapter Eleven

Sanity is highly subjective.

Like anything human, it's flawed and malleable, resting but not always sleeping, quiet in coma but never silent, and always altering.

You know you can kill, so at least you've learned something. It hasn't been a complete waste. Even as your mind races and your nose begins to burn with the sex stink, and you try to paddle away on the carpet, but a weight holds you firmly in place. Knowledge is power.

Fury made him its own. With his spine wracked by a single prolonged shiver, Cal lay there on the floor considering the black and white patterns of the bedspread, the drenched pillowcases, lampshades askew, all that sweat dripping down a bare ass he knew so well, the coitus-tangled hair curling in every direction.

Caleb's muscles decomposed into jelly, until he was paralyzed with his head weighing more than his life. It kind of felt good, actually. Everything gave out at once and he dropped back to the floor with a thump so that he wouldn't have to watch anymore.

Within a few seconds, though, somehow his body became his own again. He gave one great shirking mental heave. The rage shifted inside him like an animal crawling up from a lower depth. It cuddled against him and died—and its rot changed into something as fluid as fuel and as solid as sharp carbon. Rose was so right about what this moment was equivalent to. It couldn't have hurt worse if they'd slit his throat.

He could almost hear the tips of knives sinking into his flesh until there wasn't much left to cut. The sensitivity receded into a dull ache that left him with nothing but cold reason and clarity.

We had plans to go to the carnival tonight. There were never any invitations sent. That's why the others aren't here. This is a private party. Hand-picked attendees. The ass-kissers, the cock-suckers. Blinking twice, he was alarmed to discover he had no tears. Oh wait, there they were. *And this was why Jo didn't want me here tonight, why I was prodded to go out and get drunk.* His pulse slowed, sweat drying across the back of his neck.

Where's Rose? Was she here somewhere, outside in the snow, watching his defeat? Did she think he deserved this for what Willy had done to her? Had she followed so that she too could understand the meaning of academia? The red sheen of his sight thickened. He viewed the room through a pair of eyes he didn't own.

These revelations took him perhaps three seconds longer than it took Jodi to finish trembling from orgasm with the dean.

You knew this time had to be coming, though. You're smarter than this and the signs have been there. If not in your subconscious, then at least in the ephemera, the slow glide of the dead flowing across everything you've seen and done today. Today has been special. Today you've been shown that you are not that special. You've been brought into the fold.

Clarissa continued kissing him. Nerves ran riot under his skin, but at least that was natural. Alive with tension, his hands clenched and unclenched of their own accord. Jo grabbed the corner of the sheet and wiped the dean's face, and finally noticed Cal crying on the floor.

Come, you spirits. He eased Lady Dean aside and got up, watching Jo's body twitching with guilt, sexed and unsexed. But really *sexed*. Her gaze drained like a dead battery.

Jodi gasped like a hooked fish, hyperventilating now as her mouth worked without sound. She started sobbing, or something like that, and her groaning became a low crooning that built to a choked wail. It wasn't loud enough; Cal waited for her to really get into it—and then she was screaming, but not very loudly. The dean ought to give her a gold star for this, that wasn't asking too much. Jo's lips trembled without meaning while she cried, backing away further until she was cramped at the top of the bed into a little huddled ball, as if Caleb had come this far just to kill her. As if he hadn't already been killed.

The lady's hands found him again. *She's played this game many times before,* he thought. *She's brought others here to them, other students, other teachers.*

Trying to snap Jo out of hysterics, the dean pulled her to him, enveloping her in bone, wrapping his inhumanly long arms around her waist. They looked like they could go around her three or four more times. It was something incredible to watch, grotesque yet fascinating. Cal could not possibly imagine ever seeing an uglier naked man.

He'd always halfheartedly believed that she

occasionally slept with other guys; he could more or less live with the concept so long as it remained unconfirmed. To find that it was true, in this way, with his . . . foe . . . whatever the hell the dean was—his own girl with his enemy, now that hit the heart. His cut-and-dried ethics had already laid down in the dirt, waiting to be buried. If he'd had any in the first place. Jo stared at him as the dean shushed her and smothered her face with the wet slurps and nipping teeth of an animal that needed to be put down.

Caleb collapsed and vomited.

Clarissa laughed quietly, rubbing his back, the heels of her hands soothing the pain that was nesting, then hatching, at the back of his skull. You would never have believed it, to be touched like this, it felt so good at the moment. He was glad she was there. The heaving hurt like hell, as Jodi moaned woefully and unfurled from the dean's gangling limbs. She attempted to hide herself in the crook between the nightstand and the bed, having learned from the dean about how to bend yourself into a bucket. Tears dripped off her eyelashes as she tossed up her arms to cover her face.

Jo pulled the sheets off the bed and hauled them over her head until she was completely out of sight.

Cal shakily got to his knees, then stood and faced Clarissa. "Why?" he asked again, knowing there wasn't an answer good enough.

"I thought we could all have some fun, my dear cherub," she said. "Don't be such a killjoy."

He thought about what he would like to do: where he would stack the parts neatly, lay the heads, how he would clean up the mess. "Oh, I will be," he whispered. "I will be that."

"You're silly."

"And you're crazy." The red persisted to obscure his vision; sheets stirred and shifted haphazardly, as if Jodi was performing strange unnatural rituals beneath it. "Why are you doing this? What did you do to her?"

Lady Dean came as close to frowning as she was capable. "Nothing you haven't done yourself." She finished taking off her dress and walked over to where her husband rested on the bed, with his hand outstretched to her.

The scene looked so well rehearsed that Cal actually giggled. Two short *huhs* and nothing more.

Silently, with the rage so perfectly contained within him—no worthless shrieking or threats, why bother with all that useless shit?—Caleb moved. Hatred oiled the machinery now, and it was so much better than constantly grating against his conscience. A cold, condensed fury packed the cavity left behind in the fracture.

He flew forward and brought his knee up toward the dean's groin, hoping to force him to make a sound, give a confession, plead for mercy. Jesus, that would be beautiful. It would almost be worth it all. The dean nimbly stepped aside without any rush—so languidly, it seemed, tediously, yet so unthinkably quick—so that the momentum of Cal's leap launched him onto the bed. He rolled and bounced against the pillows, feeling the juice left behind. Jodi cried out under the sheet. Clarissa dove on top of him, laughing in his face.

"You," he snarled.

"You," she cooed.

You can come within an atom of an aneurysm, the molecular structure of murder in your hands.

"Jesus, God." He came *this* close, shoved her away, and ran.

Chapter Twelve

Wires caught by the breeze whipped against metal brace poles, clanging out riffs of loneliness.

He liked the tune. Chains rattled as wooden shutters of the carnival booths slowly whined open and slapped shut, echoes receding like footsteps stamping across the snowy banks.

The field filled with ghosts.

Circe came at him in all her forms. First as the angles of Jodi's face before he managed to turn them aside, meld them into someone else. The marionette danced around him, ribbons hanging from the sky tied to her wrists, her abdominal tract torn open with organs slinking free. And then as the dead Sylvia Campbell, or whoever she might truly be, black and white and in pencil. *Me. Sy. C.* They all wove around him, bumping shoulders as they peered over at him as if they had better things to do, those shifting slashed mouths muttering at him and groaning. The nun stood there with them, separate but also a part of the pack, praying for them all.

Icicles hung like stilettos aimed at the heads of any trespassers. Tappings and whispery rustlings of cloth were the works of seances taking place in the gloom. Other noises too, indistinguishable and drowned by the flapping of the larger tents. Posters and flyers, candy wrapper and cups and other trash from the previous night kicked up the frozen escarpment. Now it was garbage spinning past the black calliope and shadows of empty rides. Moonlight gilded the Ferris wheel. The woods crackled.

Caleb looked out at the carnival.

Ghosts lacked the proper spirit. They didn't frolic at their appointed hour, resting calmly in flux beside him. You just couldn't trust anybody. No haunting sirens called, no blind men waited on hand to relate funky prophecies. It was time for somebody to tell him something, but his sister and the various Circes never did manage to actually get anything out. Night was as numb as his fingertips.

Completely unlike himself—and for the first time in years—Cal made an effort to reach for memories of his sister. He thought that perhaps she, of anyone in his life, would understand the sorrow of what he felt now. The moment he started, the nun left him. She didn't want to be reached, he saw that now. It wasn't really equitable, what had happened to them both, but it was close enough. For a long while he stood in the field without moving, and he knew his eyes were the same as hers. Not much more than slashes.

The carnival had come up from the deep South. They'd fouled up and overestimated the warm air masses that had cleared their path from Alabama to Kentucky, and the permission paperwork they'd needed in the last three towns hadn't cleared properly. In order to make up for the losses they'd been forced to play towns in the middle states that they'd never hit before. Now they were stuck much farther north in the winter than they'd ever intended to be. But they set up anyway, and made the best of it. They'd play one more town before swinging back down South before the rainy season began.

Tents waved and billowed in the wind, some of them buckling beneath the weight of wet snow. The carnys couldn't stay out here in their rigs the way they usually did; they were forced to crash at the cheapest motels in town. The caravan of trucks and vans paraded through the center of town each day and would for another week. The concession stands and game booths remained locked. The blizzard had driven mounds of snow up against the Ping-Pong ball pitch, hall of mirrors, test your strength games. Painted signs could barely be made out through the heavy sheen of rime. The fun house didn't look like much fun.

His wrath burned a blue flame. He thought about what Willy would say, and how Rose would react. Maybe she'd forgive him and wouldn't bother to twist the blade in even farther.

Fruggy Fred would have an answer to give, but would it be the right one?

His sister brightened, then faded. Perhaps he had finally lost her, or she him. How she must have hated him for being the younger child, for having missed what she'd had to endure. He couldn't imagine being held down in the back of a van, repeatedly violated while they scratched and bit your belly, and after the doctors pulled out the stitches you came home to find some brat watching cartoons and eating cookies. He felt extremely lucky that she hadn't decided to garrote him in his bed.

Perhaps that was why she'd chosen to relate

the graphics of trauma to him, a child who could be nothing more than a sounding board of stupidity. It would've been something if she'd known back then what would happen in his life, and instead sought to protect him from that loss of faith. If she'd been trying to pass on a lesson, he hadn't learned it well enough. Maybe to her, sitting in the bathtub with her knees squeaky clean, this kind of sharing had been a form of love.

"Hey!" someone shouted behind him.

Cal jumped, and his knees nearly went out again. He wheeled and stared in disbelief, watching Melissa Lea McGowan walking toward him across the field, trudging down the hillside, a long scarf unwound to her hips.

"Hi!" she called out happily, her petite body bundled in a ski jacket, her face outlined by the hood tied under her chin. Melissa Lea carried a different atmosphere with her across the deserted field, too buoyant in the swell of ghosts. Her smile was out of place here, and it felt like even the shadows were irritated by the intrusion. As if there hadn't already been enough laughter tonight.

"I thought it was you just standing there." One curl from her bangs stuck out from the hood, and she carelessly flicked at it with the back of her gloved hand. "Well, you certainly

are dressed nicely tonight, Mis-tah Prentiss.
What's the occasion? Where are you coming
from, eh? Hmmm?"

Doing the Yok didn't make him smile. He
thought he might throw up again, except he'd
been pretty much cleaned out. He recoiled from
her as she came closer, remembering how she'd
also spooked him outside the window of the
storage room, watching. "That's twice you've
done that to me."

She grinned. "Couldn't wait until breakfast?
Seems we can't get rid of each other."

"No, we can't."

The clanking of metal-on-metal further underscored the desolation of the dark. Melissa
Lea picked up on his sour mood and moved
closer, concerned already. "I'm sorry, Cal, I really didn't mean to startle you. It's a beautiful
night, but I guess it *is* kind of scary out here."

"Are you following me?"

"Following you?" She moved to him until she
saw the look on his face, and whatever was
there was enough to make her stagger back a
step. The snow crunching under her boots
sounded like bones breaking. "I don't understand."

"Of course you don't."

"What are you talking about? I was just out
walking."

"Yes," he hissed, trying to get the word out from around his gritted teeth and listening to it hurtle toward her. "Out this late in the freeze, this far from school, by yourself. But . . . are . . . you . . . following me?

"Huh?"

"I'm not a great believer in coincidence, Melissa Lea. Especially not tonight."

"You're—"

"So why are you trailing me?" He couldn't call it paranoia any longer. This was necessary; he had to protect himself any way he could. "Are you just another one of *them?*"

She stepped back another couple of feet. "Another one of who? What kind of a ridiculous question is that?"

"From where I'm standing it's a pretty smart one. See, I've always asked a great deal of questions, but I never received too many answers. That's been my fault, I finally realize that." The slashing wind chafed his cheeks, cooling the burn a little and holding the fire at bay, but he was into it now and couldn't stop. "So how about if you just answer me?"

"I'm not following or trailing you, Cal."

"No?"

Her smile came down like an elevator with the cables cut, eyebrows rising into angry inverted *V*'s, those beautiful lines scrunching and

217

zagging. At any other time he would have thought it was cute. Her gaze drew him to it again, and he still wasn't ready for it. "No. What the hell's gotten into you? I just saw you standing alone and thought I'd say hello. Don't be so suspicious."

"Am I?"

"Yes."

"Then what are you doing here?"

Melissa Lea frowned even more deeply, furrows obscuring the smooth skin of her forehead, lips thin and white. He could see she was getting scared of him and he didn't care much. How far did Bull tell him date rape had risen? Thirty-five percent? "I don't have to tell you a damn thing."

"No, you don't," he said. His shoulders and back throbbed. He wondered if Willy would have been able to lay a finger on the dean, if it just took more muscle mass to catch the scrawny bastard. Tree limbs heavy with ice snapped off in the darkness. "But tell me anyway."

"You're freaky tonight, Cal."

"Well, yeah."

She gazed steadily at him, breath leaving pouches of white in the air. You didn't know; maybe the dean had somebody left behind, in reserve, to do his bidding. You could never tell who that one last deceiver might be. She looked pissed, panicky, and playfully mischievous, as if deciding whether it was worth the effort to battle through his hard shell, or simply turn and make a run for it. Her frown untwined slightly. She studied him for another minute and cleared her throat. "Okay, Mis-tah Prentiss, I will tell you, if you've got to know.

"Fear death—to feel the fog in my
      throat,
    The mist in my face,
When the snows begin, and the blasts
      denote
    I am nearing the place,
The power of the night, the press of the
      storm
    The post of the foe;

"And if that's not reason enough for an unbeliever in coincidence to believe, then how about if you listen to this . . . ah, 'At midnight in the quiet' . . . no wait . . . it's silence, I think. Yeah, it is . . .

"At midnight in the silence of the sleep-time
    When you set your fancies free,
Will they pass to where—by death, fools think,
      imprisoned—"

Tom Piccirilli

It sounded like Byron, the great lover.

She jutted her chin out at him, as if daring him to take a poke. "Now, as a fellow humanities major, you really ought to get the hint, Cal."

"Ought to, but don't."

"Like I said, I don't owe you an explanation."

"Nope," he admitted. It didn't matter much anymore. The fury continued to condense until it was only a knot of energy in the center of his chest, fiery but under control. If they had wanted to finish him off, they'd failed. So far. If Melissa was here to do him wrong, she couldn't; there was no more wrong to be done, for the moment. They'd probably be coming at him for another try, but that wouldn't happen for a while yet, and he'd be gone by the time they got around to it. If she was a friend, then he needed her, but he wouldn't leap for the bait. Either way, he was about as ready as he could be.

She said, "I was working on my ENG 135 paper, cooped up in my room footnoting and cross-referencing all afternoon, until I finally slogged out into that lousy blizzard for some dinner." Clearly she resented giving him details, but he could tell she was having a little fun too. This was a mystery, and she enjoyed working through it. "When I got back to my room I took a nap, and when I woke up I was feeling all groggy and heady with poetry, you know what

I mean, and I grabbed my Norton anthology off my shelf and read for a while and got hooked on the Victorians again. My roommates came in arguing about politics, as usual. I couldn't work anymore and I was getting claustrophobic listening to them squabbling so I read at the library until it closed and then I took a walk. That's it. A simple walk. Here I am. Want a signed affidavit? A note from my mother? Or are you going to lighten up now?"

She didn't have a backpack or any books. It hit him again that she might be lying, that from the beginning she had been watching him, but he couldn't hold on to the fear or anger anymore. The lady and the dean couldn't do that to him. Someone was dead, but it wasn't him.

"Was that Byron?" he asked.

"No, Robert Browning."

"I liked them. I'm not familiar with the poems."

"No reason why you should be unless you're writing a paper charting his poetic style before his marriage to Elizabeth Barrett as opposed to the evolution of his work after marrying her."

"Was there any?"

"I think so. The first piece was the opening stanza of *Prospice*, and the latter from the epilogue to *Asolando*, his last published volume."

Something loped beside them in the thicket

and Melissa Lea swung around nearly into his arms. He still had his hands in his pockets and didn't take them out. His arms had been too full tonight. He could hold on to wraiths but not to flesh. The moon glowed, pale illumination washing over the ice. She turned to look at him, and the interest he'd felt for her this morning started a slow crawl back up his throat. His girl lay under a sheet like something in the morgue. That beauty mark at the corner of her eye grabbed his attention again.

His ghosts hadn't helped him.

Maybe she would.

Cal held out his hand to her, reaching for a last chance. "Come on. Maybe I can win you a stuffed animal."

"No," she said. He wasn't sure if she was going to tell him to go take a squat. Her laugh sounded on the edge, like it could go either way. "No, you can't. The games are always rigged."

Chapter Thirteen

Change clinked together as he tossed his last two quarters on the counter of the carnival game booth. Four wrinkled dollar bills lay nearby. He gripped the worn hide of the softball and rubbed it between his palms until the friction warmed his chilled fingers. Wind slid sharply against his hackles.

"And you actually caught them together?" Melissa asked quietly.

Caleb didn't bother to nod affirmation—talking about it hadn't been a venting for him. It had been nothing. At least he'd finished his sentences. The ache hummed a lullaby, got him nice and cozy and made him want to snuggle down into the new mattress. Redemption might be waiting for him there. The content of his dreams would be warped with Jodi trembling in the bed with a carcass. Fruggy Fred completely believed the legend that if you died in your dreams the shock would stop your heart. Caleb didn't want to take the chance.

"You should've punched him out."

"I tried. I couldn't even lay a finger on the slithery bastard."

Standing sideways behind the counter, he concentrated on putting all his strength and effort into the pitching motion—rolling his shoulder and extending his arm, lifting and stepping, pivoting his hips, just as Clarissa had done in her dance. Maybe he'd learned something after all.

The three milk jugs set atop each other forming a pyramid were weighted and rounded to keep them from falling over no matter how hard you threw the ball. Maybe it was just another calculus problem. The trick, he thought, was to strike the jugs at the bottom exactly where the weights were. Testing his theory had cost him a few bucks, but he was getting the hang of it.

He remembered Professor Yokver doing cartwheels down the aisle, screeching, "I am not moving!"

Well, sometimes you had to call a cheat, a

cheat, and then step back and see what happened.

Melissa Lea sat on a high wooden stool behind the counter, with his overcoat wrapped around her small body like a comforter. "And you say they planned it that way? Some kind of kinky exhibition so you would find them in the act? What kind of sleazoids run this school?"

"The best."

Winding up, Cal lifted his left leg and tightened his arm, waiting for the moment of release. Now that he knew just where the lie was, he could aim for it. The cool, friendly bitterness held nothing back as his elbow cracked painfully, loud as a rifle shot. He straightened his arm and hurled the pitch with all the force he had, the flame inside him surging as if hit with oxygen. The softball flew and struck the bottom milk jug squarely where he'd intended it to hit. The jug slid back another inch and teetered to one side, tumbling the other two cans as it crashed over.

There was something highly moronic in feeling any satisfaction from this, but he didn't much care. "About time."

"God, that must have hurt."

"No. Not really." He massaged his arm. "Well, yes."

"I didn't mean your elbow. I'm talking about

what happened. I'm so sorry for you."

He went to the back of the booth and grabbed the two ugly stuffed animals that the owner of the Softball Haven hadn't locked up in his trailer with the rest of the prizes. "I know what you meant, Melissa."

"Oh."

In his left hand he held a teddy bear with only one eye, a missing patch of fur on its cheek, and a green felt tongue almost ripped off. In his right fist he grasped the toy cat without a fourth leg, no tail, ears chewed off—the thing looked like a pack of dogs had been at it.

Still, they were enough. They had to be. It seemed ridiculous to have smashed the links of the flimsy chain with a rock, only to leave six bucks of piddling change behind in order to feel honest about taking two disgusting and worthless stuffed animals. But the dream had to remain pure, if nothing else. Every guy should win a pretty girl a toy at the carnival at least once in his life. He'd sworn to do it, and now he finally had.

"In the movies they're always a lot bigger and nicer," Cal said. "Directors like moments like this, scenes where the guy offers his girl a present, pinnacles of drama and romance." He pinched the nose of the less ugly of the two—the cat, he thought—and put it in Melissa's lap.

"See, sometimes the dolls are full of diamonds or drugs, and then a killer stalks the heroine home to get the doll."

"You say the sweetest things. I think I'll risk it." She picked up the mangled cat and stroked its ratty whiskers. "Oh, Cal," she whispered.

It wasn't a sighing, *Oh, Caaaal,* with valentines popping out of her eyes. Merely a nice show of sympathy. She reached over and ran her fingers through his hair, stroking the back of his neck. He jerked away.

Melissa Lea held the cat and made it dance and meow along the counter of the ball stand. She had it pounce onto his chest and kiss his face. "*Mwa mwa mwa.* Kiss kiss. Nah nah boo boo. I really do like you, Cal. I know this isn't a particularly good time to tell you something like that, but I had trouble putting two cohesive thoughts together while doing my paper today."

"Why?'

"I couldn't stop thinking about having breakfast with you tomorrow." The cat nibbled his ear.

That begged the same question. "Why?"

At least now he had a chance for an answer, even though the word made him think of the lady, hanging over him and trying to lick away his soul.

Melissa Lea shrugged. "You're cute. Hey, I'm

sorry to be so bold. I don't want to complicate your life even more, but I thought I'd be honest."

"Good."

"I'm also pretty damn scared about what this says about our university. You can have them brought up on charges, I'm sure. Called before a review board. Maybe even tell the cops."

"The mayor was at the party."

She peered at him, and he realized he couldn't blame her that she didn't fully believe him. It all sounded like exaggeration, a bizarre conspiracy. Then again, shit like this was pretty common. Priests taking advantage of altar boys, high school teachers getting pregnant by their students. Who the hell knew what else was happening every day out there?

"What does it say?" she asked. "About how it's probably happened before, how normal it might actually be, you know, perceived by these kinds of degenerates." She sat back on the stool. "Is it, Cal?"

"I don't know." He considered telling her that he'd be leaving in the morning but couldn't find a way to get it out. The secret would be safe so long as it was inside him. He tore off the rest of the teddy bear's tongue and flicked it away. All he could truly trust was the overwhelming sense of just how stupid he felt. And even that sounded dumb. He didn't know how to explain just how bad a student he'd become.

"I'm glad you're here," she said.

"Sure."

"I mean it."

The vapor of her breath touched him. The shutters of the Softball Haven clapped heavily against the wooden planks at the side of the shack, and she jumped. "I'm glad you're here with me, Melissa." It was the truth—a small part of it—and he guessed it should be said aloud, though the truth didn't have as much meaning as it did before tonight. "Was meeting you just a coincidence? Twice today?" Especially considering that he'd never even noticed her before.

"None of what happened back there at the dean's house was your fault, Cal. You've got to believe that. It makes no sense for you to feel guilty about it."

Of course it was his fault, as much as theirs, because he should have known better. The Yok had gone to such lengths to hammer in the instruction, until it had become a private joke. He could imagine Yokver and the others grinning, thinking how easy it had all been, how you could hold the text right up to his eyes and he still couldn't see the facts. Four years of this and he still hadn't picked up on it. He wondered if he should just go and get it over with, sleep with the lady and let all his hostility out, get good and vicious so he could graduate with honors.

Caught by the breeze, the teddy bear's tongue whisked over his shoes. Mrs. Beasley and Kitty Carry-All wavered briefly in the moonlight. Maybe his sister was still out there, but she must've been dodging him now. Cal wished for what everyone eventually comes to wish for— the chance to start over somewhere earlier down the line, with a little more sense, a few more nerves less tightly wound. But he never thought it would happen so soon, at only twenty-one, and already wanting to go back and try it again a different way. He could leave, and he could live, but he could no longer see where there was left to go.

He asked, "Do you think your roommates are still squabbling?"

"Well, one is a poli-sci Republican who thinks the Reagan Administration was composed of the best minds since our Founding Fathers drew up the Declaration of Independence. The other is a liberal arts major who quotes from Timothy Leary and Abbie Hoffman, and refuses to believe they're dead. See, Leary had his head frozen even though his body was turned to ashes and shot up in the Space Shuttle. She's memorized the greater percentage of the transcripts from the trial of the Chicago Eight. She also thought Bill Clinton looked good running in those sweatpants."

"No way."

"Yeah, they're pretty weird. Quite possibly they'll battle until dawn. They have before."

"Okay, let's go back to my room, then."

She hopped off the stool and the cat kissed his chin. *"Mwa mwa mwa.* Nah nah boo boo. I thought you'd never ask."

Chapter Fourteeen

Someone had taken the time to wash Cal's bloody handprints away, thank Christ.

The new kid at the security desk sat there in his seat nodding off, his shaggy red head tilted back on the fulcrum of a pencil neck but perking up when he heard them walk in. He'd grown threads of a silky rust-colored beard in an attempt to cover his acne-scarred skin. He wasn't having much luck.

Bull must've put the girl with the Walkman on probation and let her out before the end of her shift. This kid was the best so far. He checked Cal's university ID right off and asked Melissa Lea to sign in, then took her identification and promised to return it when she left the dorm.

In his room, blocking her with his body, Cal made sure that his closet door was shut so Melissa wouldn't see the his bloodstained coat and sweat socks. The stink remained strong, though she didn't seem to notice. She shrugged off her coat and folded it over the back of his chair, took the stuffed cat from her pocket and carefully perched it on the ledge of his desk. The cat was a weird attraction, and kept bothering him: a toy meant for Jodi, earned yet also stolen, displayed like a medal by another girl. An ending of sorts, but without any closure. All this dreaming, for a stuffed animal.

Melissa Lea turned and stared at him curiously when she saw the busted phone and the spilled peanut butter on the floor. He explained about the crank calls, and kept to the lie about the dying dog. "It hasn't exactly been the best of days."

"Goddamn, I guess not."

"Sorry." Shit, he'd done it again.

"You don't have to apologize for that, either." She kneeled and started to sweep up the plastic shards of the phone with the side of her hand.

"Be careful," Caleb said, moving to her, "there's glass." She let out a paltry pained snort, and he saw droplets of blood welling between her thumb and index finger. "My fault. I should've warned you sooner. I broke a jar of peanut butter this morning."

She held out her hand to him. "Not your fault. A couple of tiny slivers; see if you can grab them with your fingernails." She sucked air as he took her wrist and removed the glass splinters. "Hurts like a paper cut."

You could do this, if you wanted to. Let go of everything else and start slowly, start fresh. These were the elements of romance. The light touch, the yearning for friendship and comfort. You haven't forgotten how to smile, even if it does feel like the tendons in your cheeks have been rusted. There was still plenty of time before the morning. You didn't have to keep the nun on your back.

Dried blood discolored the handle of his socks drawer, but she didn't see it. The peach wall seemed to be a strikingly similar shade to Melissa's flesh tone, blood underneath skin, and he wondered how pale or pink Sylvia Campbell had been. He could only see her in black and white.

He said, "Hold on, let me—"

"Do you have a Band-Aid?" she asked. A titter balanced in her voice. He grabbed his shaving kit out of the top of the closet, opened it, and removed bottles of hydrogen peroxide and rubbing alcohol, a box of cotton balls, a handful of gauze pads, some tape, an Ace bandages, and a couple of Band-Aids in a variety of sizes. For someone so prepared to bleed, he should've seen the damage coming.

"It's not open-heart surgery, Cal."

"Suffer your pain in silence, will you?" he said. "If you're a big girl, I'll—"

"You'll what?"

He was about to say *kiss your boo-boo*.

Huh. He almost couldn't believe it. Will you just look at that: a joke already, making with the eenie-weenie mindless banter. Hell, that didn't take long to bounce back from, not at all. You can live through just about everything.

"Nothing," Cal said.

"Maybe you'd better give me a bullet to bite." He swabbed the two small cuts clean and applied the Band-Aid. She wriggled her finger and nodded.

"Still works?"

"Thank you, Doctor." She righted the phone, replacing the receiver in the broken cradle. "I think it'll still ring, but you won't be able to call anyone. Most of the buttons are missing."

"Just as well," he said. He would be gone in six hours, and no one would know. She shrugged and nodded again—not exactly em-

235

barrassed, but something nearly as uncomfortable as that. With some distress he discovered that he couldn't stop staring at the beauty mark.

It was getting bad again. His fixation with phantoms was starting to slip over the side of the living world. If only he'd had this sort of dedication when it had counted. What next? Become a stalker? Draw his own little pictures of women's faces and slip them between the pages of paperbacks? Couldn't he just enjoy the next few hours with Melissa and not go slowly wading into the deep end? He didn't think he had the discipline yet.

Standing in the middle of the room, equidistant from the four walls, as if they were dead center on the deck of a rocking boat, they each took a shuffled half-step toward one another. She let out a casual sigh when their toes touched.

The bed, for all its significance, remained only a bed as he studied Melissa Lea in the same slow manner he tried to examine poetry. There was so much to be seen there if you could find the subtext in the expression. The laugh lines of her face were like stanzas that might hold consequence in his life.

They lay back on the bed, relaxing. The new mattress wagged around and the springs uncoiled with the squeakings of foreplay as she turned on her side, trying to get cozy. He put his arm around her and she touched him. Her eyebrows were pinioned in a constant look of bemusement. She yawned.

Silence kept them company. It was all right now. No words attempted, not even with their hands or other body language. A difficult trick at times like these, but they were making it work. A half hour passed as he thought of ethics and failure and all that fit between. Melissa Lea's breathing became slow and rhythmic, and when he glanced over he saw she was on the verge of sleep.

Someone's dead. He hadn't forgotten.

She snuggled up to him with her fingers gently resting on his thigh. She was one of those people who exhaled through their mouths while they slept, her moist lips quivering, going *brrrr* like a baby in a bathtub making motor boat noises. It was good to know she lay alive beside him; he nestled his ear against her thick sweater, the way he'd done with Lady Dean's mink, listening to her heart beating, much faster than Jodi's constantly slow and steady rate.

Feeling the warmth of her body against his skin helped him to hate. There was less pressure to face circumstances now than if she'd waited for him to make the effort to unclothe her. Sharing the muteness was proper and perfect. It reminded him of his relationship with Fruggy Fred.

He plucked at the covers, smoothing and drawing them back. He couldn't shake the sight of Jodi hiding under the wet sheets, ready for a ritual burial. The cat on the desk stared at him.

Tentatively touching Melissa Lea's belly with the back of his wrist, he turned aside. It took a few minutes for him to notice, with some repugnance, that he'd already reached out with his other hand to hold it against the stain on the wall. They were creating some kind of circuit. Coitus.

Man, you just had to be fucked in the head.

Windows hummed with gusts of wind.

He caught himself about to mutter, and the phone rang.

He'd done a good job smashing it. The bell inside clinked hesitantly and gurgled. He lifted his chin in the direction of an anguish he always felt when something called to him in the middle of the night. If it was Rose, he wouldn't be able to talk her down from the precipice, and if it was Willy, he might hiss out all he felt until the guy's eyes started to drool onto his cheeks. He knew it wouldn't be Jodi.

Melissa murmured, "Huh?" She rolled toward him and tried without success to interlace fingers with him.

"Nothing," Cal said in her ear. He brushed hair out of her face, and liked doing it so much that he put the hair back and brushed it away again. You went with it when it was good. She let out a long breath and settled deeper under the blankets. He slipped over her legs and off the bed, then greedily snatched up the receiver before it had a chance to warble again.

"Hello."

There was only emptiness.

It didn't surprise him. Caleb clenched the cord and twisted it around his wrist, the hinges of his jaw tightening until they hurt, and then tighter still. His back teeth ground together in the crunching of bone and filling as he leaned forward a little, altering his stance, ready to leap if he had to.

And like the other times, during these past hours when he'd answered to this inertia, he strained and listened closely to the silence, patiently trying to fight through the blustery freeze waiting on the other end.

It wasn't Clarissa; he would have heard the giggle, the eminence, or the dean's slickness. He didn't know how to defend himself from the void of whatever called to him and wasn't sure that he wanted to. Funny to still be thinking of it like a movie playing out. Now the girl was getting up and wiping the fake blood off her tits, the director calling for a reset, the makeup man having a great time as he swabbed her chest and then dappled on the new paint. There was more too, a film within the film, documentary-style. He saw it clearly. Visions of the decomposed bodies of his parents wanting to speak with him, to warn him about his sister, as her mottled form in the bathwater moved spastically across the tiled floor.

Silence swirled in biting circles.

Each of the other times he'd been cranked he'd somehow tried to make friends with the audience, hoping to appeal to their mercy, just before the rage hit. It had been the wrong play to make. He just had to go inside.

"It's okay," he gently urged. "You can say it. Talk to me. Answer me."

"Cal . . ."

The voice was unique in its lack of resonance, with a lilting cadence you only hear on hospital deathbeds.

It was Fruggy Fred, asleep.

That made sense, of course, though he didn't totally grasp what it might mean. Fruggy, dreaming, calling him over and over. The questions of his senior thesis, infinite in their subtleties and connections, came back in one solid punch to the rib cage. *The Death of Circe,* the sorceress, the dreamer. The book sat in the bottom drawer of his desk. The cat glared at him.

Cal turned. Cold sweat exploded on his forehead. "Fruggy. It's been you all the time."

"Me," Fruggy Fred whispered.

"But . . . but . . ." The barbs pulled in his throat. He did his best to mimic Fruggy Fred's monotone, swallowing his panic. "You've been coming into my room to sleep here, haven't you? While I've been out?"

"I—"

Take it easy. Slow, slow, don't jar him loose. You just had to go inside. "Where are you?"

"I'm—"

"Are you in your room?"

"No."

"Where then?"

"Here."

"At the radio station?"

"Here."

"Where are you? Come on, you can tell me."

He could just see Fruggy lying there, sweating in bed and lost all the way down in his own head. Fruggy Fred groaned a little, his tongue slapping hard against his teeth as he sobbed, *"I'm in Hell."*

Caleb eyed the wall, understanding. Yes, you certainly are. We all are. Beneath the stain lay a girl with her hands splayed over the edge of the mattress, strands of her hair puffed against

241

the exhalations of her *brrr* noises, looking
nearly as slain as any other murdered woman
who'd slept in his bed.

"What is it, Fruggy? What else is Sylvia saying?"

Only the hint of a sound lost in a lolling rush
of air. ". . . "

"What?"

After nearly a full minute there came the
same wafting sound, ". . . " Cal held his breath
and concentrated, focusing. He closed his eyes
and tried to reach backward into the darkness
of his skull. After another minute he felt his
lungs ready to burst but still kept digging himself inside as far as possible, like going into the
grave. His ears burned trying to catch the tail
of Fruggy's message from the other side of
sleep.

". . . ock . . ."

Cal took a deep breath and did his best to
keep from panting. "Yokver?"

Only silence.

Without deciding whether he believed what
he was thinking, if it might be the truth, he
asked, "Did the Yok kill her, Fruggy?"

Something broke within Fruggy Fred then; a
lessening of pressure, perhaps. His sleepwalk
persona seemed to suddenly grow more accus-

tomed to acting in the body. "I talked to her, Cal."

"Yes."

"I did what you told me."

Jesus, God, which one of us is more crazy?

Caleb's heart twisted to one side, the implications sending chills rippling across his back. Melissa sighed. He thought he saw a shadow outside his window but realized it was only his own jerking motions, as the cord wrapped tighter and tighter. "What did she tell you?"

"She only wanted an education." Fruggy Fred seemed to find that funny, the slightest edge of laughter coming on. "Lied to her. Killed her."

"Why?"

In the recesses of that inflectionless voice crept heartache and awful sorrow. "She taught them."

"What did Yokver do with her?"

"She's still so strong," he wept, as much as he could now. "She won't leave me alone."

Cal rubbed his face in frustration. "You've known about her all semester long, haven't you? You could smell it too."

"I—"

"Since you came in here on that first day and fell asleep on my bed, in the spot where she died. You knew. She's been trying to get to me through your dreams, hasn't she, Fruggy? . . .

243

hasn't she? . . . and you've been calling to let me know."

" . . . "

"You know we're insane."

"I know that, Cal." Fruggy snorted as he cried. "Angels dream."

"Oh, Christ." Caleb's legs wavered, and he held on to the desk for support. He looked over and watched Melissa Lea dreaming, and saw his own hand moving in his line of vision as if it were no longer a part of him, touching her lightly on those moist lips. "What does she dream about?"

"She says she dreams about you, Cal." The emotion became stronger in his voice as Fruggy came closer to stirring. "Don't go back there." And again, as if imploring, terrified, screaming and awake, ". . . ock . . . !"

Fruggy Fred grunted in pain.

There was the sound of thick splashing.

The phone went dead.

Caleb's hands began to pour blood.

Chapter Fifteen

Professor Yokver's house, like the man himself, stood with enough scorn to raise bile.

The moon cast something other than light down upon it. You could feel the infection. Diseased trees grew unchecked over the front yard in quilted, cross-hatched, cancerous patterns. Branches jutted like twisting spears, lancing the sky, scraping into the broken, snow-stuffed rain gutters, and driving down against a roof full of loose shingles. The lawn was an assemblage of gullies and ditches, the perfect place for hiding bodies. Even the snow looked fake, too many shades off from being white. The house was a disgrace, but that didn't matter much. The dean kept Yokver close, but not too close.

Tom Piccirilli

Cal stood in the street, his tie still tight and straight, the London Fog flapping. From this spot he could see all Professor Yokver's darkened windows: the grungy brass knocker and the weather vane reeling. Turning a half-step to the right, he looked down the block and saw the far-off lights still burning in the dean's bedroom. All the luxury cars were gone from the area: the mayor, the school board, the other officials who influenced the university had been sent home well fed and sated.

Jodi was still in there.

His father's tiepin weighed heavily upon him. The man had quit school at sixteen, and Cal should have followed suit. Worked in a sheet metal factory, joined the union, started putting into Social Security, punched a time card for forty years. Right now loading beef in a meat locker for the rest of his life sounded swell.

Cal had grabbed the cotton balls and Ace bandages and bound the stigmata before the wounds sprayed too much all over his room. He'd been careful not to awaken Melissa Lea, even while tying knots in the bandages with his teeth. He left her snoring in his bed and pulled the blankets over her shoulder, kissing her on the forehead, like the brother he'd never really had the chance to be.

Blood proved blood.

Fruggy Fred was dead.

Numbness prevailed. His sister was talking to him again, brandishing a crucifix, her habit undulating. He watched, knowing what was about to come, as the rat heads bit their way out of her torn robes. She teetered this way and that in the wind, struggling to stay up but beginning to bend beneath the weight of the crucifix as the rats ate through her. He watched, fascinated but a little leery of the obvious symbolism, until she moved off, dragging Christ in the dirt. It probably wouldn't be such a bad idea to see a psychiatrist one of these days.

He wished the soul of Sylvia Campbell would put in another appearance; she only had to show up for a second, give him the good word. Anything; a silver outline whisking past the porch, a banshee shriek urging him on. It would have helped. Siren song lamenting, the moon goddess throwing stones. Anything.

But the red-mouthed Circes were gone and he was alone, standing beyond the curb staring at Yokver's house. The Ace bandages worked better than he'd expected, soaking up the blood and stanching the stigmata. Considering how long it took to heal the other times, he was sure the holes in his hands had already nearly finished closing. He heard the bells ring five. He'd be out of here by dawn.

Drifting, he shut his eyes and thought about what a long day it had been. If, in fact, these hours only comprised one day, and not his complete existence. Something had come full circle in that amount of time, beginning and ending in the push of birth to death. Maybe it was him; maybe it was only a nightmare that was him.

So what was he supposed to do now? How did it all fit? . . . Could the screaming puppet truly be a murderer, or had he heard Fruggy wrong? . . . Cal waited, hoping to see the Yok scurrying back from wherever he'd left Fruggy Fred's massive body, his hands wet with mud. Sylvia Campbell had wanted an education and died for it. Fruggy had told him that and died for it. Someone else had been killed, he knew, but Jodi was safe and would be forever. Caleb wished he was back in his coffin.

The light in the dean's bedroom blazed in the distance, mocking him with impunity.

Even after all the vomiting he could taste the Four Roses he'd slammed back in the Owl, and could still hear Candida Celeste asking him with extreme annoyance, *What is your problem, you asshole?* He sniffed the breeze, catching evergreen and mint fragrances. A few crackling leaves rolled in the gutter.

Caleb unwrapped his hands and let the bloody cotton wads and bandages fly into the street. Wind carried them across the frozen ditches until they flailed into the trunks of gnarled trees, waving like streamers. His palms were perfect again, lifelines back in place. He slowly walked to the curb, echoes of his footsteps snapping but soft as the clicking of poker chips.

Stepping up Professor Yokver's snow-covered sidewalk, he moved toward the house. No footprints in the snow of the front yard. Bushes leaned forward scratching at his coat, leaving ice crystals against the back of his neck. He searched for signs of murder and found none. Gazing at the brass knocker engraved with the name YOKVER, he put his hand on the doorknob and turned it. At first there was a slight resistance, but he forced it and heard the lock rattle free. Cal walked in.

He slipped through the darkness, not caring which direction he took. A light was on down the hall. Carefully picking his way around the furniture, padding like an animal, his breathing became shallow. He could feel the rage lurking in his chest, just waiting to cut loose.

Odors here were outrageous: eggs and sausage, cabbage and boiled ham, as well as lilac room freshener and useless pinches of potpourri. He couldn't smell Fruggy Fred's corpse. Either the Yok had no sense of smell or he enjoyed the wild fusion of stench. It must've excited him, reminding him of whorehouses and the stinking long hallways of the specialty clubs, the backrooms of the strip joints where the lap dancing ran to five hundred bucks a throw. Cal could just see him in this place, grading papers and setting up a course outline, sniffing and humming.

A noise from another room.

A book closing with a deliberate thump.

Cal's nostrils flared. He tried to take in the whole house, dissecting the scents to discover clues in the air. Mirrored reflections of his movements brought his gaze to an antique cabinet. Yokver, the lady, the dean—they all liked to look at themselves. Cal understood that PHILO 138 was designed for some other purpose than to teach ethics. To weed out the weak, and take advantage of whatever flaws could be discovered. To gather together the creamy next generation of useful children. They rooted out Jodi's incessant need for perfection and put it to use, laying claim to her distress. Educating her. If she'd ever mentioned it to him, could he have stopped it from happening? Would he have even tried?

The light from the room threw a yellow glow into the corridor.

Cal proceeded to the doorway.

Slowly rounding the corner, he glanced inside: a study, shelves bulging with books and statuary. His temples throbbed painfully, his eyes attracted to the burning ersatz oil lamp with the green metal shade. He checked sidelong from there until he saw the glint of pearly teeth. They were set in a sick smile that wolfishly leered at him from behind a desk. Yokver lifted a gun from his lap.

Cal nearly burst out laughing.

A gun, right? He couldn't believe it.

"What is good?" Caleb asked. The window in back of Yokver afforded a nice view of the dean's house, the bedroom as bright as if it was on fire. "What is evil?"

With a frown, Professor Yokver said, "You were almost finished, too."

Sometimes you just wanted to roll around on the floor hugging your sides while you laughed until you passed out, and then when you woke up you wanted to do it again.

Cal's lips melted into a rough smile. "Finished, huh?" He supposed it was true, one way or another. "I admit it, I really *have* learned a lot from you today."

"Yes, but like most repressed, maladjusted orphans you walk through life discarding each profundity you chance to find."

"Low blow, Yok."

The gun wavered with a displeased gesture. Maybe Yokver was serious and maybe he was just playing a wild card. The guy definitely had an obscene need to fantasize. So did Cal. No wonder they'd been drawn together into this match; it was bound to happen.

The Yok didn't have his glasses on. He didn't need them. "You were a perfect candidate."

"I see."

"Afterward you would have been offered a position at the university."

"In what capacity?"

"As a professor of humanities. As an instructor."

"And I flunked?"

"Yes, unfortunately."

Leave it to Yokver to keep going on like this. Unfolding the master plan, not even realizing how ridiculous he looked and sounded. You could stand here all day just shaking your head and smirking, but eventually, if you wanted to get anywhere, you had to fall into the same dialogue.

"I suppose this is when I sneer at you and shout, 'You're insane.' "

"Not necessarily." Yokver waved the gun aimlessly, the ponytail bobbing. "You see, poor boy, you've been going steadily mad for some time now." A laugh escaped from one of them.

"We've all gone through the process."

"Uh humm. Process?"

"The learning process. The creative process. The shattering, and the promised ascendancy."

Cal nodded. "Oh, that process."

"You would have made an excellent teacher." The Yok grew more exuberant, putting a little flourish in his wrist as he wagged the gun, as though needing Cal to understand the concepts that would be illustrated by his demise. He looked like he wanted to get up and run around the room like a ballerina, one of those chicks who throw rose petals all over the place.

"Kill me," Cal said, "but for Christ's sake don't make me listen to you." Statues of literary icons faced him from all over the room. A bust of Poe with a raven on his shoulder, somebody who might've been Nietzsche, maybe Kafka, framed portraits of Flannery O'Connor, Sylvia Plath, Charles Bukowski. They'd seen their share of corruption and depravity too. Cal spoke calmly, knowing already how it was going to end. "You make it sound like it's acceptable to do what you've done, using students just because some of them are scared or lonely, or weak or simply young. Or just really dumb, like me." It was okay to admit it because now he saw the light. "The dean took advantage of Jodi's fear to hold a lock on her grades. That's not the creative process. Call it what it is: extortion. There's nothing brilliant in it. You're all just a bunch of pimps."

"Not so."

The Yok smiled, and slung himself forward as if to give another exhibition of how there was no such thing as movement. Papers fell to the floor, and two bookends that formed a bust of Shakespeare teetered at the edge of the desk.

Yokver had played the role for so long that it had become a part of him. He probably couldn't even distinguish anymore between himself and what he had created, what had been built around him by the lady and the dean. Anywhere else and the Yok would've simply been a degenerate in a dirty bookstore, poring over pictures of chicks with dicks. Watching the girls in the glass booths, pumping quarters in so he could get off thirty seconds at a time, talking into a microphone and telling them to spread, play with a plastic banana. Here, though, they put him to good use. A position of respect and authority, where he could squeeze brains until they bled black juice. The efficiency, at least, could be respected.

"I was wrong to think you were a clown," Cal said. "I realize my error now."

But the thing of it was that Yokver truly remained a clown, one of those nasty ones that come after you in your nightmares. You just know that for every ten jesters in the world there was one lunatic hiding behind the greasepaint just waiting to bury the steak knife in your eye.

"Yes, too late, I'm afraid. All the more tragic, too late. I had to peel away the outer layers. All that dead skin left behind on you."

"The scales falling from my eyes?"

"That was the hope."

Cal pursed his lips and looked down at himself. "To expose what stands before you now."

"Well, the plan went slightly awry. You're much more neurotic than I ever could have imagined." Yokver chuckled, but Cal could hear the fear. "You see, poor boy, you were already on the verge of either suicide or progressing into a sociopath. The game revealed this deficiency in you too late, alas."

Cal didn't mind the word *game.* It was accurate enough, and he could try to think a move or two ahead now. "Where do you people get off the psycho train?"

"See here, poor boy—"

"Stop calling me that. Where's Fruggy Fred?"

"I don't know to whom you are referring."

"You wouldn't lie to me now, would you?"

"No, there is no purpose."

"Then I'll ask you an easier question—"

"Tut, I am becoming bored."

No, he wasn't. Look at the way he was swallowing. Yok was trying desperately to seem ready, to go all the way with this, but it was only the act he cared about, not the commitment. In another five minutes he was going to be on the floor crying. "How did you know I'd be coming here tonight?"

"I was informed of your failure to perform up to Clarissa's expectations, and of your unwillingness to accept the, ah . . ." A snigger now that started low and shallow and wound up sliding off the deep end. The gun did a bit of a jig in his hand. ". . . position that was offered to you. It made perfect sense that an aberrant like yourself would seek to cut down all his demons in one fell swoop."

Cal almost wanted to talk about demons for a while, get out a notepad and list and number them, get all the names straight. He never thought for a moment that Yokver wouldn't answer all his questions. "Why did you kill Sylvia Campbell?"

"I found her, the lovely creature, and gave her the identity by which you evoke her, allowing her entrance into the university."

"What a guy."

"I inducted her among us."

Without urgency, Cal moved forward, and Yokver raised the gun a bit higher, aiming between Cal's eyes. "So, is that what you did? Explain it to me."

"Why should I waste the effort? What's the point?"

"Educate me, Professor. Tell me who you are."

But he already knew. There wasn't any reason to be shocked, and he felt foolish for ever having gotten upset. You've got nuns being raped in the backs of vans, gym teachers nailing cheerleaders under the bleachers, cops robbing banks, eight-year-olds strangling two-year-olds—you just had to figure the time and place would come along where they'd give you an *A* for some hanky-panky and then slit your throat.

"We are guidance," the Yok said, and he managed to sound earnest.

Fruggy Fred's words came back; he'd known it all along. Cal said, "Whoever controls the dreams of the world controls the world."

Yokver's eyebrows fluttered. "I never took you for a poet, Prentiss. No matter who you quoted you never had the heart for verse. It always dripped out without any substance. All treacle and no value. Poor crippled boy. Sensitive lad, if you hadn't been cuckolded you probably wouldn't even care right now. I knew they were taking it a step too far."

"Yeah, at least a step."

"Pity."

The Yok had his own weaknesses too, so clearly defined now that Cal knew what to look for; he'd been shattered once upon a time, all right, and Cal heard the broken pieces rattling in that snigger. "You've never been with her, have you?"

"Who?"

"You know."

"No, I—"

Cal couldn't help it and finally let out a belly laugh. All of this, and the sick bastard hadn't even gotten to dip his stick. "You've never had the lady." Look at the reaction as the Yok showed his teeth, pain scrawled in his eyes, all the masks stripped from him now, one after the other peeled away like skin off an onion. "Poor Yok. You haven't felt those lips, never smoothed yourself against her heat."

There, in the window behind Professor Yokver, teacher, dictator, guide, puppet, creator of new sensibilities, and lousy worm burrowing in the mud, came the sign Caleb had been waiting for. An outline in silver, a banshee wail and the siren song. Moon goddess throwing down stones.

All of that and more, as he watched the dean's bedroom light go out.

The end of the night class.

"You're the one who needs to be taught a lesson," Caleb said. "Circe will instruct you."

"Circe?"

"And the nun. They're here now."

Yok trembled wildly. Cal's eyes were separate graves as he leaped and shifted in the same motion. His muscles cording, overcoat unfolding like wings, his face remaining as lifeless as a corpse's. The shot retorted like a tree branch cracking.

Caleb hefted one of the Shakespeare bookends and drove it through Yokver's head.

Chapter Sixteen

The black house, wind rising.

Knowledge flowed through his bones as the darkness drew back, shreds of blue and yellow appearing in the sky. He'd made it until morning. At least he'd gotten this far. For some reason he considered that an achievement. His sister might be proud that the rats hadn't taken him down. She could be softly applauding his efforts. Blood had always been with him, in him and on him. He was able to dismiss most of his thoughts but not the feelings, pulse hammering, hackles raised like quills. Once again he stood in the street and watched. Caleb as killer.

There was nothing to see except the dean's

home, dark and silent, where he'd left the pieces of himself on the floor.

He stroked the tie and fingered his tiepin. His stomach lurched, tightening further, the way it did for final exams. He couldn't catch his breath out here in the charcoal gray minutes before dawn. He felt a little drunk and warmth flowed through him. Quickly, he trudged through the snow to the back of the house, skirting the piazza until he found himself in front of the set of glass doors again.

They would never lock these; of course not. That would be too full of middle-class mentality and fear of burglary. They'd always feel safe.

The glass door slid back in its track. Caleb entered.

He could smell his own vomit in these halls.

Along with tomato juice, orange juice, a lot of scotch and vermouth. Tables and mantels in the parlor were covered with empty wine and champagne glasses. The maid's night off. The room was more quaint than threatening, now that the crowd had gone and taken all its dirty politics.

Inside the breakfront were a half dozen crystal figurines mixed among the Dresdens. Rainbows swirled inside them as sunlight edged across the shelves. Colors pirouetted. He touched a pair of dancing ballerinas with the edge of his finger. A rose morning lit the window. There was something girlish and innocent about the figures, as though they were leftover shards of Clarissa's own childhood. Words rang: *We've all gone through the process.* Cal rubbed his eyes. Impossible to picture Lady Dean in pigtails, playing with Barbie dolls or jumping rope, or doing anything not precisely controlled and impeccable.

Thinking of babies, one of his heartstrings pulled taut, and he felt an instant of pity. He and Jo had rarely spoken of children. Did it mean he was finally ascending; would he pass this test? At least this one? The hydrocephalic kids never had trials like these, and they smiled a lot more.

Someone shuffled behind him.

Cal whirled and threw a fist wildly in the direction of the sound, hoping to make contact with the dean's lengthy bones, nail the slippery fucker once and for all and splinter him in one blow.

He missed and overextended himself. Pain flared in his ribs as all the air was forced out of his lungs. Fingers like iron turned him around, gripped under his armpits and squeezed, lifting Cal up onto his toes. Powerful forearms wrapped around the back of his neck in a full nelson. He continued to struggle and was bashed into the sideboard for his efforts, the figurines crashing to the floor.

Bracing himself as best he could, he brought up the heel of his shoe and kicked backward into somebody's knee.

"Ow!"

Did he do it? Had he nailed the dean and made the prick finally say something? Cal kicked again and missed.

"Would you relax!"

"Oh, no."

It was Willy, wearing sweatpants but nothing else, squinting and disheveled from sleep. He looked weary in the way a man like him could only become after a long bout of sex. The rest of the pieces slid into place faster; who was here, who wasn't, who'd already been taken out and why. Willy didn't have a goddamn clue.

Bending and massaging his knee, he frowned at Cal, shaking his head. "You've got to be kidding me. What the hell are you doing, sneaking in here like that? Do you know what time it is? Are you nuts?"

Yes, and you had to be, if you wanted to make the grade. *Is everyone I know a part of this?* "Jesus, God, what are you doing here?" He already knew the answer but couldn't help asking.

"You'd better split," Willy said. "It's a long

crazy story that you won't want to hear now. Believe me, really. This definitely isn't your scene. Go on. Leave now, Cal, and I'll catch you in the morning."

Caleb could only mumble, "Willy." There was no way to explain all the circumstances of this night, the difference between good and evil, if there was any. Cal was now a murderer and couldn't quite admit that it was a bad thing. Willy appeared so boyish and innocent, acting protective, that an animal mewl of pain worked up Cal's throat. He had no way of letting his friend know what their school years were really meant to harvest, especially now that they'd produced it. "Clarissa?"

Willy groaned and rolled his eyes. "No, Julia Blanders, man; that's who I was talking about today. Listen, I was failing English, even if I did read *Catcher in Your Eye*. She promised me a good creative writing mark, you know, and it's all subjective anyway. Rose found this story with my name on it. She knew I didn't write it, thought some freshman piece of ass did it for me; that's when she went hysterical. I'll straighten it out with her this afternoon, trust me."

"Listen; you've got to listen—"

But Willy couldn't hear him. "Funny she wasn't here tonight, but thank God she didn't come. You'll get a kick out of this: See, then, the dean's wife, she starts coming on to me . . . amazing, listen, I'm telling you . . . you shouldn't be here . . . I threw out your invitation; I knew some kind of shit like this was going to happen—"

Willy trying to insulate Cal, and the lady going after him when Cal wouldn't dance. It was his fault.

"Rose," he gasped.

He could see it. Rose rushing around the campus, berserk, wailing and flapping her arms wildly, going to Julia's office and throwing Willy's faked story on the desk. She wouldn't have let go with the questions, those nails out ready to tear at somebody's eyes. She went in thinking Willy had a girlfriend in class, grilling Julia until she figured out he was sleeping with his professor. It couldn't have been difficult; Julia was already settling into their ways. Rose hauling off and slapping her face; that was how Julia had gotten the bruise on her chin. Look at how things added up when the scales have fallen from your eyes. Rose wouldn't have stopped, the state she was in. He imagined her picking up a chair, grabbing a letter opener. Julia running around the room and both of them screaming until . . . until security came.

Until Rocky showed up.

"Aw, c'mon, man," Willy pleaded. "Don't give me those puppy dog eyes and more of your lectures, all right? She'll get over it. She always does. I know she was hurt, but there's more to it than just that. If she doesn't, then maybe it's time to split up anyway. Trust me, hey—"

"Jodi." The name was unfamiliar now.

Willy crossed his tremendous arms and sighed. Willy's voice remained strong and resonant, in control and sort of enjoying the way the situation was unfolding. He could revel in it, treasure his new status. "So you found out about everything, huh? Now you understand what's been happening, but it's all okay. Don't go crazy, man, don't hate her. Don't hate me either. It's just a little fun. It's just another form of give and take, but instead . . . ah hell, my grades can be made or shit-canned. I need to graduate. I don't want to stay here forever like you do."

"I do?" Cal croaked. Willy didn't know anything, and at the same time knew it all. He'd understood from the beginning about the real class, the true test, but had failed it anyway: he cared about sex but not enough about his education.

"You're hurting now because you know Jo's been screwing around, but you have to realize that everybody does it, more or less, excluding maybe you. And I'm not too sure about you, except maybe you do it politely."

"Listen, Willy, you—"

But how could you say it so that he might believe you? The words wouldn't come. Cal had slowed down too much and now couldn't get it back up to speed. The reek of Yokver was still with him, dragging him down. Cal tried to reach for Willy's shoulders, but he felt too awkward, unable to move. He saw what Julia had always written on his papers, *awkward* in red letters tearing across his pages, and she must've known he'd eventually come to this moment.

"It's nothing to get riled about. Go home. Have a nightcap. Get some sleep." They all wanted to put him to sleep. "Let it go for tonight and I swear that tomorrow everything will be a whole lot better. Don't hold it against her. You know what medical school means to her."

Willy stood there, his physique faultless, self-reliant and assured in his sexuality and power. *He thinks he's living out the fantasy of being a gigolo.*

Cal whispered, "You don't know what you've gotten into."

"Me? You're the one who—"

Yes, he'd been the one. His naïveté and ineptitude had sent everyone around him straight into the dean's bony arms. If only he'd kept his eyes open. If only he'd listened to his sister while she lay there wet and finished, murdering herself.

And now more shadows filled the darkened halls behind him.

Cal had been wrong to return. Fruggy had told him not to come back and he did it anyway. They would have kept Willy on because he was ignorant of the facts, too wrapped up in his own pecs and abs, but now—Christ, now they'd make the play right here in the room, everybody getting impatient with these spiraling events, and he'd see for himself what this night class truly taught, and finally figure out that Rose and Fruggy were dead.

"Get out of here!" Caleb cried, shoving Willy toward the glass doors. His friend's muscular frame barely shifted. Willy didn't know what was behind him, simply standing there with a puzzled grimace, thinking Caleb crazy, of course, but oh, this time, this time . . .

Willy died with that look on his face.

The force of the bullet blew him backward against the wall. Cal watched it unfold in a hideous freeze-frame effect—as if Yokver had at last been proven right, that there is no such thing as motion . . . one, two, three languorous center shots; the killer took his time, placing them in a tight triangle as Willy's blood pumped out of his chest and spattered the sideboard. He remained standing, though, legs quivering; they weren't going to take him down easily.

Unable to focus his eyes, Willy glanced here and there, and then here again, settling on Cal. He tried to raise his hand and plug his finger into one of the holes but couldn't lift his arm high enough. Cal wanted to do the same thing, raise up his bleeding hands now, place them on Willy's wounds, and let his own blood pump into his friend's veins. Willy took two more unsteady steps, legs beginning to falter, a weak smile tugging at his lips as a gush of black blood burst from his mouth.

Caleb reached for him, sluggishly, everything still so languid and awkward.

His fists continued spurting as the nail holes opened even wider this time, the final time. He could see the shining tiles of the floor through his palms and wished more than anything that there was some pain. A scream wrenched from his throat, trying to catch Willy as he finally dropped, but with all that blood he slid from Cal's hands. Willy crumpled.

His torso convulsed while Cal cradled his head. Then nothing.

Jodi let out a yelp.

"Shut your filthy mouth," Lady Dean told her.

Caleb looked up.

Rocky stood in the middle of the room, his security guard's uniform the color of his hair, his gun the color of his eyes. No real facial expression there. It was worse than dead, and still not entirely satisfied. Fruggy hadn't been saying *Yokver*. Fruggy had been begging *Rocky*.

Others stood behind him, naked or in sleeping attire. Jo wore the teddy Cal had bought her for her birthday, now ripped, with one strap torn by teeth. Terrific. Clarissa with only black stockings on, bruises on her back and belly as well, welts matching Jodi's. The dean's lack of flesh gave them no buffer. He stood in his "Father Knows Best" togs, satin robe and slippers, for Christ's sake; all that was missing was the pipe and a dog named Fauntleray at his shin.

"You suffer from hysterical stigmata," the lady said, astonished and smiling, still looking as though she wanted to take him to bed. Would anything ever wipe that expression off her face? "Remarkable; you've taken your martyr complex to the extreme." Her tongue flicked over her canines, fingers roaming her thigh. He understood that she would've liked him to bleed on her too. "You're far more insane than we'd ever thought."

"Yokver agreed," Cal said.

She hovered near Willy's feet. "What a waste." Her stockings glowed in the dawn, hair a tumble of knots, snarled by the hands of her devotees. "He was a fabulous lover."

Jodi was down to the dry heaves and had the decency to drop to her knees and waver as if she were about to pass out. She'd better do well in medical school, all right; she'd better work the ER every night for fifty years in an effort to make up for all the lost lives.

The worst part was that he didn't really blame her: living in a tar shack with the retarded babies and an alcoholic mother and touchy-feely white trash brothers would drive you to extremes too. Caleb had nothing left to give. He spoke and was amazed to hear something very similar to his father's voice coming from him. "There was no need for this."

It was puerile but honest. Like his dad.

Lady Dean sashayed forward, really working it, putting in some *wockachicka*. Jodi kept her gaze on Clarissa, taking pointers maybe, so she could practice the swing of those hips later, when she used it on the doctors. "His girlfriend suspected. Fascinating how quickly suspicions of the subconscious can come to the forefront. Especially when one is directly faced with the thought of losing one's love to another. Perhaps there truly is no worse emotional pain."

"There isn't."

"They had to be eliminated, my darling

cherub, and you only have yourself to thank for that." Her voice had a soothing quality, melodic and soft, and even now he enjoyed hearing it. "As Jodi informed us, when Rose arrived in such a state at her room this afternoon, you admitted to your friend's adultery. If you'd sought to placate her with a lie, there was a chance she could have lived. Instead, she rightly assumed that Julia was his lover and chose to sift through certain files, discovering discrepancies in the grading system. She taught us a lesson."

"Good."

"All it would have taken was for you to lend a soft shoulder to cry on and a few encouraging pats on the back."

"Yes," Cal said. "I see that now." He stared down at the dwindling flow of blood from the holes in Willy's chest, though his hands kept up a steady stream.

The lady held to her role as much as the Yok had. Each gesture timed well, the lift of a wrist, the tilt of her head. He kept looking around for a director sitting in a high chair somewhere, giving orders. She hadn't escaped academia. It had molded and crushed her into form, swallowing her into its stone walls and hallowed halls, sucking out her marrow as much as it had anybody else's. In a few more years it would beat her down until nothing was left but bone and loose skin. He recognized it truly, and it gave him a little satisfaction.

She asked, "And Professor Yokver?"

"Gone to a better place."

She was genuinely intrigued, smiling so wide that he saw the film on her tongue. "You've quite a murderous streak, my cherub."

"You aren't kidding," he said. Jodi whimpered, and the dean slapped her hard. He could leave marks on her now.

"Don't you want to ask about your fat friend?"

"I already know why Fruggy had to die."

Rocky eased his gun back into the holster, knowing Cal wouldn't run. He'd only fooled himself into thinking he'd ever had the chance to flee. The simple fact was that he didn't want to leave. Rocky drew a finger through his crew cut. "I had to leave him in back of the radio station. He's too goddamn heavy to move."

Maybe Bull would find the corpse and finally act on his hunches. He'd realized Rocky was involved in something ugly but couldn't quite figure out what. Or if he did know, he didn't want to believe it.

Another long pause, and a charge passed between Clarissa and the dean. For the first time Caleb caught a hint of real respect between them.

"Because he was absolutely brilliant," the

lady said, no smarm in her voice. "He understood what no one else could. He knew where real power lay, and fought it with the most peaceful and passive resistance imaginable. He was too strong an adversary to leave alive."

"He's not gone; he's still here. Along with Circe and my sister. You can't get rid of any of them."

Maybe she'd thought he'd finally cracked and paid no attention. She was wrapping up her speech, enjoying the denouement. "And this way we can dispose of them all together—in an auto accident, perhaps. The fire will do wonders to eradicate evidence, including bullet wounds. No autopsies will be necessary. All good friends, out on a winter's night."

"Quite nicely tied together."

"Not perfect. But perfect enough."

"Why tell me all this?"

"Because there's still a chance to save you."

That snapped up his chin. He wanted to scream and he didn't want to scream. There was a frantic giddiness swirling around in his belly trying to get loose. If he gave in to it, he'd wind up rolling on the floor until they kicked him to death. He said, "No, there's not. But tell me who Sylvia Campbell was, anyway."

Clarissa uncharacteristically answered without prodding. "A prostitute." He must've made a noise because she said, "You find that hard to believe?"

"Not really."

"Our Professor Yokver was quite given to primal urges, but the ugly little man always chose to pay for such services rendered. He was full of his own neuroses." She gestured with her fingers like moths. "Merely a tramp who wanted to get out of the gutter." Jodi's face grew even more ashen. "He promised her just such a chance. She was quite accustomed to paying for favors with sex, and following whatever role was assigned her." He didn't want to think about that. Circe in pigtails and knee socks, calling the Yok Daddy one day and dressing up like Little Bo Peep the next. "An inordinately sad girl for her age. Perhaps almost as sad as you."

"Perhaps."

"Once she realized that the relationship would widen and evolve she sought release from her studies. Her duties."

"Boy, you people never get off the fucking stage, do you?"

Clarissa had tuned out his lines, as if she was trying to hit every mark, facing the all-seeing audience of the university. "Who would think that a common whore would have such integrity?" A throaty laugh filled the room.

275

Cal whispered to his many ghosts, "I'm proud of you." And he was. It was they who had taught him something about life and death, the will to fight against your fragile fate, to take matters into your own bleeding hands.

"Our fair Yokver became so sentimental about her loss that he even refused to part with her belongings. That was a foul mistake."

"Why did you put her in my room?"

A shrug that jounced her breasts flawlessly. "Consider it an experiment in behavior. I wanted to note your reaction, to see if you could be trusted to enter our circle."

"And?"

She came over and ran her index finger over his lips, tugging at the corners of his mouth before pressing down on his tongue. She pulled out her finger and licked it like a cone. "I don't know."

He hoped Jodi at least still loved him a little. As if he had always expected betrayal, he looked at her with a grin and some forgiveness, as much as he could spare now. He wasn't too surprised that his grade in the night class had yet to be given. That depended on the final exam. The dean laughed with malice, reached out with his skeletal, elongated hand and grabbed Jo by one arm, violently shoving her forward. It was important that she watch this and learn from the quiz, however it played out. She dropped to her knees again, her hands feebly reaching for Cal. The dean pulled something from the pocket of his robe. A flash of morning sunlight glinted off metal. Cal couldn't tell if it was a knife or a gun, ruler, scissors, pen or medal. He stood and felt the crystal shards crunching under his shoes—there was an analogy to be made between their lives and the pieces of Dresden.

As the smiling dean stepped closer, a cadaver coming closer, Cal wondered if Melissa Lea would find his thesis in the bottom drawer of his desk and hunt down the truth behind the death of Circe. He hoped she still dreamed. He wished he knew what had been used to sacrifice Sylvia Campbell: a Bowie knife or a meat hook, a scalpel or an ice pick. Their smiles took form in the dawn. Circe and the nun milled among them, frantically waving their slashed arms, trying to get his attention. Maybe there was time for one last lesson. Clarissa looked as if she might kiss him, start dancing with him, and proceed with his training. He did not know if he had passed the final. Cal could read nothing in her face. The dean kept smiling and stalking closer, perhaps to welcome him into the fold, or maybe only to get a better angle for stabbing.

Outside, a green van would be parked in the street, waiting for him.

Not caring much if he survived the next moment or not, if he had joined their circle or failed the night class—as the razors of his education continued being driven into place—Caleb realized that whether this was life or death, good or evil, he had, despite all else, completed the course.

THE DECEASED
TOM PICCIRILLI

Something is calling Jacob Maelstrom back to the isolated home of his childhood—to the scene of a living nightmare that almost cost him his life. Ten years ago his sister slaughtered their brother and parents, locked Jacob in a closet . . . then committed a hideous suicide. Now, as the anniversary of that dark night approaches, Jacob is drawn back to a house where the line between the living and the dead is constantly shifting.

But there's more than awful memories waiting for Jacob at the Maelstrom mansion. There are depraved secrets, evil legacies, and family ghosts that are all too real. There's the long-dead writer, whose mad fantasies continue to shape reality. And in the woods there are nameless creatures who patiently await the return of their creator.

___4752-7 $5.50 US/$6.50 CAN

Dorchester Publishing Co., Inc.
P.O. Box 6640
Wayne, PA 19087-8640

Please add $1.75 for shipping and handling for the first book and $.50 for each book thereafter. NY, NYC, and PA residents, please add appropriate sales tax. No cash, stamps, or C.O.D.s. All orders shipped within 6 weeks via postal service book rate. Canadian orders require $2.00 extra postage and must be paid in U.S. dollars through a U.S. banking facility.

Name_____
Address_____
City_____ State_____ Zip_____
I have enclosed $ _____ in payment for the checked book(s).
Payment <u>must</u> accompany all orders. ☐ Please send a free catalog.
    CHECK OUT OUR WEBSITE! www.dorchesterpub.com

HEXES
TOM PICCIRILLI

Matthew Galen has come back to his childhood home because his best friend is in the hospital for the criminally insane—for crimes too unspeakable to believe. But Matthew knows the ultimate evil doesn't reside in his friend's twisted soul. Matthew knows it comes from a far darker place.

___4483-8 $4.99 US/$5.99 CAN

FOUR ORIGINAL NOVELLAS BY

BENTLEY LITTLE
DOUGLAS CLEGG
CHRISTOPHER GOLDEN
TOM PICCIRILLI

FOUR DARK NIGHTS

The most horrifying things take place at night, when the moon rises and darkness descends, when fear takes control and terror grips the heart. The four original novellas in this hardcover collection each take place during one chilling night, a night of shadows, a night of mystery—a night of horror. Each is a blood-curdling vision of what waits in the darkness, told by one of horror's modern masters. But as the sun sets and night falls, prepare yourself. Dawn will be a long time coming, and you may not live to see it!

THE HOUR BEFORE DARK

DOUGLAS CLEGG

As children, they played the Dark Game.

When Nemo Raglan's father is murdered in one of the most vicious killings of recent years, Nemo must return to the New England island he thought he had escaped for good and the shadowy farmhouse called Hawthorn. But this murder was no crime of human ferocity. What butchered Nemo's father may in fact be something far more terrifying — something Nemo and his siblings have known since childhood.

"Here comes a candle to light you to bed . . .
And here comes a chopper to chop off your head."

—A SPECIAL HARDCOVER EDITION!—

THE INFINITE

DOUGLAS CLEGG

Harrow is haunted, they say. The mansion is a place of tragedy and nightmares, evil and insanity. First it was a madman's fortress; then it became a school. Now it lies empty. An obsessed woman named Ivy Martin wants to bring the house back to life. And Jack Fleetwood, a ghost hunter, wants to find out what lurks within Harrow. Together they assemble the people who they believe can pierce the mansion's shadows.

A group of strangers, with varying motives and abilities, gather at the house called Harrow in the Hudson Valley to reach another world that exists within the house. . . . A world of wonders . . . A world of desires . . . A world of nightmares.

SECOND CHANCE

CHET WILLIAMSON

You are invited to a party. A reunion of old college friends
who haven't seen each other since the late 1960s. It should be
a blast, with great music and fond memories. But be fore-
warned, it won't all be good. Two of the friends at the party
weren't invited. In fact, they died back in college. But once
they show up, the nostalgia will turn to a dark reality as all the
guests find themselves hurled back to the '60s. And when they
return to the present, it's a different world than the one they left.
History has changed and the long-dead friends are still alive—
including one intent on destroying them all.

BARRY HOFFMAN
Born Bad

Three apparent suicides by coeds at the same university seem tragic, but not particularly frightening—until the police receive a mysterious letter claiming responsibility for the deaths. Suddenly the police and the university find themselves caught up in a deadly game of cat-and-mouse as they try to stop the killer before another innocent victim dies.

Shanicha was born bad. She was born with no compassion, no remorse . . . completely heartless. She's become a brilliant puppet-master who plants the seeds of destruction, then sits back to watch the evil she has wrought. To Shanicha, other people are merely pawns in her cruel game . . . a game she plays to chilling perfection.

THE NATURE OF BALANCE
TIM LEBBON

One morning, the world does not wake up. People lie dead in their beds, killed by their own nightmares. They're lucky. For the few remaining survivors, the new world is a confusing, terrifying place. The balance of nature has shifted. Mankind is no longer the dominant species–it is an intruder, something to be removed, destroyed by an Earth bent on vengeance.

Blane is a man on his own in this world gone mad. He has no distant memories, only the vague certainty that something momentous has happened in his past. Fay is enigmatic, dangerous, a dark witch and a player of gruesome games. What roles will they play in nature's new era? And will they be able to survive long enough to find out? Will anyone survive?

UNDER THE OVERTREE
JAMES A. MOORE

Can you see them, the faint shadowy forms that move through the woods near Lake Overtree? Have you noticed what's happened to Mark, a once lonely young man whose entire world is mysteriously shifting to accommodate his desires? The girl of his dreams is his for the taking, the kids who bullied him are disappearing one by one, and even his stepfather has started treating him like a real son. Can you hear the screams of the damned, of those foolish enough to cross Mark's path? Listen carefully. The world is changing in terrifying ways. It's all happening ... Under the Overtree.

GERARD HOUARNER
ROAD TO HELL

Max is a man. An assassin, to be exact. But within him lurks the Beast, an unholy demon that drives Max to kill—and to commit acts even more hideous. Throughout the years, the Beast has taught Max well, and Max has become quite proficient in his chosen field. He is an assassin unlike any other. To put it mildly.

But now Max has a son, an unnatural offspring named Angel. Through Angel, the spirits of Max's former victims see a way to make Max suffer, to make him pay for his monstrous crimes. And while Angel battles his father's demons, Max himself must try to escape from the government agents intent on capturing him—dead or alive.

SERVANTS
OF CHAOS
DON D'AMMASSA

The isolated little fishing village of Crayport, Massachusetts, might seem almost normal at first glance, but appearances can be deceiving. You would never be welcome there. Outsiders never are. The inhabitants of the village are unusually hostile toward strangers, and you might notice some of them share an odd physical trait. . . .

If you look very closely, though, you might discover the hideous secrets of the mysterious island off the coast. And if you aren't careful, you'll meet the powerful group that dominates the town, the ones known only as the Servants. Just pray you never catch a glimpse of the Servants' unimaginable masters.
